Mystery of the Secret Code

BOOKS BY RUTH NULTON MOORE

The Sara and Sam Series
  Mystery of the Missing Stallions
  Mystery of the Secret Code

Other Junior High Books
  Danger in the Pines
  The Ghost Bird Mystery
  In Search of Liberty
  Mystery at Indian Rocks
  Mystery of the Lost Treasure
  Peace Treaty
  The Sorrel Horse
  Wilderness Journey

For Younger Readers
  Tomás and the Talking Birds
  Tomás y los Pajaros Párlantes (Spanish)

Ruth Nilton Moore

Books I have read:

- ☐ Danger in the Pines
- ☐ The Ghost Bird Mystery
- ☐ In Search of Liberty
- ☐ Mystery at Indian Rocks
- ☐ The Mystery of the
  Lost Treasure
- ☐ Peace Treaty
- ☐ The Sorrel Horse
- ☐ Tomás and the Talking
  Birds
- ☐ Tomás y los Pájaros
  Parlantes
- ☐ Wilderness Journey

Sara and Sam Series:

- ☐ Mystery of the
  Missing Stallions

- ☐ Mystery of the
  Secret Code

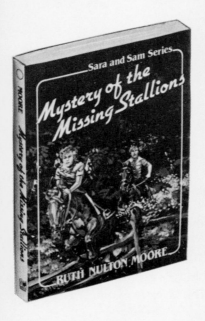

HERALD PRESS
Scottdale, PA 15683
Kitchener, ON N2G 4M5

Printed in U.S.A.

Mystery of the Secret Code

Ruth Nulton Moore

Illustrated by James Converse

Sara and Sam Series, Book 2

HERALD PRESS
Scottdale, Pennsylvania
Kitchener, Ontario
1985

Library of Congress Cataloging in Publication Data

Moore, Ruth Nulton.
   Mystery of the secret code.

   (Sara and Sam series ; bk. 2)
   Summary: Teen-agers searching for a treasure hidden
at an old farm find a secret message written in code.
      1. Children's stories, American.   [1. Mystery and
detective stories.   2. Twins—Fiction]   I. Converse,
James, ill.   II. Title.   III. Series: Moore, Ruth Nulton.
Sara and Sam series ; bk. 2.
PZ7.M7878Mzk 1985   [E]   85-5441
ISBN 0-8361-3394-3 (pbk.)

MYSTERY OF THE SECRET CODE
Copyright © 1985 by Herald Press, Scottdale, Pa. 15683
   Published simultaneously in Canada by Herald Press,
   Kitchener, Ont. N2G 4M5
Library of Congress Catalog Card Number: 85-5441
International Standard Book Number: 0-8361-3394-3
Printed in the United States of America
Design by Alice B. Shetler

90 89 88 87 86 85 10 9 8 7 6 5 4 3 2 1

To David and Lesia Longacre
with love

Contents

1

The Strange Girl

Sara Harmon glanced out the window of the school bus and drew in a long sigh. All the kids around her were laughing and chattering together like long-lost friends. Everyone seemed to be happy and excited on this first day of school—everyone, that is, except her.

The girl sitting next to Sara had completely ignored her and was leaning halfway across the aisle, talking with two other girls. In the seat in front of her, Sara's brother Sam was sitting with their friend Huy Chau, their heads together in earnest conversation, and farther down the aisle her older brother, Tim, was talking easily with Vickie Raber, as if he had known the pretty blond girl all his life instead of just the week before school started.

A flutter of uncertainty started up inside Sara. This was her first day in a new school, and she wondered how it would be, being the new girl in her class. One thing she did know. It was a strange and disturbing experience to be sitting in a school bus with nobody paying the least bit of attention to her. Back in Philadelphia, where they used to live, there had been millions of friends to jabber with on the way to school.

That summer her family had moved to Maplewood, a small college town forty miles north of Philadelphia, where Professor Harmon had accepted the position of chairman of the history department at Maplewood College. They had bought a small farm which dated back to the American Revolution and was called the old Goodwin place because Goodwins had lived there from the eighteenth century until just a year ago. Because of the pretty marsh pond in the woods beyond the old stone house, Sara had renamed their new home Marsh Pond Farm.

One of the best things about Marsh Pond Farm was that their nearest neighbors, the Rabers, owned a horse farm a half mile down the road. Sara smiled as she thought about the exciting summer they had when she and her twin brother, Sam, solved the mystery of the stolen stallions and helped Huy Chau, a Vietnamese refugee, find a foster home with the Rabers.

Vickie had missed out on all the excitement because she was in Nebraska at the time, visiting her grandmother. But when she returned, just a week before school started, Tim was quite willing to fill their pretty neighbor in on everything that had happened. Tim and Vickie were both seniors in high school, which helped further their friendship, and now Sara could see Tim's black curly head bent close to Vickie's blond one as he leaned over to look out the window at the large, two-story, brick school they were approaching.

When they had all piled out of the bus, Vickie gathered them around her, like a mother hen, Sara thought, and led the way to the office where they picked up their schedules and room assignments. Tim was elated that he and Vickie were in the same homeroom, and after they helped Huy find his homeroom and Sara and Sam theirs, they vanished with a group of seniors to the upper floor of the building.

Sam was assigned to Class 9A and Sara to 9B, right across the hall.

"I just know that 9A is full of brains like you, Sam," Sara said wistfully, regretting that they had to be separated in this strange school.

Everyone on the bus seemed happy and excited on this first day of school—everyone, that is, except Sara.

Sam grinned at her with that crooked smile of his which was hardly more than a lift at one corner of his mouth. Flipping a lock of straggly hair back from his eyes and waving a casual good-bye, he turned and walked into 9A with all the assurance of a student who had lived in Maplewood all his life. Sara watched until her twin's auburn head disappeared through the doorway, then with much less confidence she entered 9B.

The room was already filled with students standing around, talking to one another. A tall, attractive girl with long chestnut-brown hair seemed to be the center of attention. She was leaning against her desk in the middle of the room, surrounded by a group of other attractive girls. *A clique if I ever saw one*, Sara thought as she made her way past the group.

No one seemed to notice her as she slipped unobtrusively into the seat of an empty desk by the windows. All about her she caught snatches of conversation: "Did you have fun this summer? Who do you think we'll have for math this year? Is anyone going out for cheerleading?"

Everyone seemed to know everyone else except the girl who sat in front of her. Sara wondered if she was new at Maplewood High, too. She was about to tap her on the shoulder and introduce herself when at that moment the girl turned halfway around in her seat. For an instant her lips parted as though she was about to speak. Then she stiffened and turned quickly away.

Sara frowned at the girl's strange behavior and stared curiously at the back of the bent head in front of her. Oblivious to the laughter and chattering voices around her, the girl sat hunched over a book that looked as if it had come from the library. It was obvious she didn't want to talk, and Sara turned her attention to the other students.

12

So this is how it feels to be the new girl at school, she thought. It was a strange sensation to Sara, who had always been popular in her school in Philadelphia. She looked up with envy at the tall girl with the chestnut-brown hair. How long would it take her to break through that tight circle of friends? Sara wondered. Were small-town cliques even worse than big city ones?

Her thoughts were interrupted when the teacher walked into the room. The students found seats and an expectant hush settled over the class as the teacher started to speak.

"For those of you who don't know me," she began, "my name is Mrs. Bailey. I shall be your social science teacher as well as your homeroom adviser."

Mrs. Bailey had a pleasant face, framed with iron-gray hair. Sara had the feeling that she was an experienced teacher who knew her way around the classroom. Her reputation must have filtered down into the middle school last year, for these ninth-graders had respect for her and listened intently to what she had to say.

She carefully outlined their schedule for the day, and Sara had no problem finding her way around. At lunchtime she found herself being swept along the crowded corridor to the cafeteria.

The room was filled with ninth-graders, and the din was so loud that Sara could hardly think. If she were babbling along with the others, she wouldn't have been so conscious of the noise, she thought ruefully.

She took her place in line by a stack of brown plastic trays and while she waited to be served, she surveyed the crowded room, her eyes searching for Sam.

Even though they were twins and Sara shared Sam's auburn hair and hazel eyes, their father often remarked that they were alike "in a very different way." Sam was a loner

13

and more interested in books than in people, while Sara was just the opposite and had lots of friends in Philadelphia. That's why she almost dropped her tray in amazement when she spied Sam at a table, talking avidly with several boys from 9A.

He's getting acquainted a lot faster than I am, she brooded. There was no way that she could join him now.

She searched the crowded tables for a place to put down her tray. She saw Alison Heston, the popular girl in her homeroom, at an end table with the same crowd of girls she was constantly with. There was no room at that table, and anyway, Sara didn't think she should butt in without being asked. No sense making a bad impression her very first day, so she moved on to the back of the cafeteria where the tables weren't filled and put her tray down at an empty place.

As she lifted her milk and plate of lasagna from her tray, she glanced across the table at the person opposite her. She was surprised to see that it was the girl who had sat in front of her in homeroom.

Sara looked at the girl curiously as she sat down. She had a pale, sharp-chinned face framed by sandy wisps of uninteresting-looking hair. She wore a plain blue skirt and a wrinkled shirt which drooped over her skinny shoulders. She sat hunched over, as before, but this time she was nibbling a peanut-butter sandwich from her brown-bag lunch.

Sara cleared her throat. Searching for something to say, and finding nothing, she simply blurted out, "Hi!"

The girl looked up for the first time and seemed surprised that someone had spoken to her.

Sara turned her plate halfway around and started on her lasagna. Hoping to make friends with at least one girl that day, she said, "My name's Sara. What's yours?"

"Amy Goodwin," the girl mumbled, keeping her brown

eyes averted from Sara's friendly gaze.

Sara paused with her fork halfway up to her mouth. "Did you say Goodwin?"

The girl nodded and looked puzzled.

Sara went on eagerly, "Are you related to the Goodwins who used to live at the old Goodwin place?"

Amy bobbed her head, still looking puzzled.

"Oh, wow," Sara exclaimed, "I thought you were new here, but your family must have lived in Maplewood for ages!"

In a suddenness that surprised Sara, the girl's eyes brightened and she answered proudly, "An ancestor of mine built the house in 1768. But how did you know my family lived at the old Goodwin place if you're new in Maplewood?"

Sara blushed. "Does it show that much?"

A thin smile spread over the girl's pinched face. "Well, I never saw you around before."

Sara's eyes twinkled. She leaned over the table and said in a low voice, as if she had a secret to share, "I know your family lived in the old Goodwin place because we live there now."

Amy's smile quickly vanished. "Then . . . you must be one of the Harmons," she said, her brown eyes wide with surprise.

Sara nodded eagerly, anxious to make friends with this girl who had lived in the old stone house. She was puzzled when Amy Goodwin's mouth tightened and she had nothing more to say.

For the rest of the lunch period Sara tried to make conversation, but she had to do all the talking while Amy Goodwin sat in stony silence. It was a relief when the buzzer sounded, calling them back to classes.

What had come over this strange girl? Sara wondered as she filed out of the cafeteria with the other ninth-graders. Why had Amy become suddenly so quiet and sullen when Sara had mentioned that she now lived at the old Goodwin place?

Concern crossed her face as Sara made her way down the crowded hall to the next class. Maybe Amy acted that way because she resented the Harmons living in her ancestral home. But no, Sara thought, it must be more than that. Amy Goodwin didn't seem to be friendly with anyone at Maplewood High.

2

Vickie's Plan

How did the first day of school go?" their father asked at dinner that night.

"Great," Tim said with enthusiasm.

Sam grinned. "Yeah, we know why it was so great, Tim. Vickie Raber is in your homeroom."

"It'd be really neat if she were in all my classes," Tim added with a wistful sigh.

Professor Harmon looked up from his dessert and eyed his older son seriously. "You must keep in mind that you're a senior this year, Tim. I know the senior year is a lot of fun—parties, dates, and such. But remember, if you want to enter Maplewood College next fall, you have to study hard this year. It'll be your last chance to pull up those grades."

Tim sobered and nodded. "Yeah, I know that, Dad."

Mrs. Harmon patted his arm and quickly changed the subject by turning to Sara and Sam. "And what about your day?" she asked.

"My day was okay, too," Sam spoke up eagerly. "I met some guys who are as interested in computers as I am. We signed up for the same computer science course, and Mr. Harris, our teacher, said we'd be able to use the college computers for the more difficult projects. Isn't that neat?"

Everyone caught Sam's enthusiasm and nodded. Mrs. Harmon smiled at Sara. "Now it's your turn, dear."

After her brothers' glowing reports, Sara couldn't tell her family how much she missed all her friends in Philadelphia and how left out in everything she felt her first day at school. So she replied with a casual "Okay," and before any one of them could question her further, she told them about meeting Amy Goodwin.

"What's she like?" asked Sam.

"Well, I guess she's what you'd call antisocial," Sara answered. "Anyway, she just sits by herself most of the time."

"Is she cute?" put in Tim.

"Oh, Tim, honestly!" Sara said, laughing at her older brother. Sobering, she replied, "She could be if she'd do something with her hair and smile more. She acts as if she just doesn't care about anybody or anything. The only time she brightened up was when she talked about her family living in the old Goodwin place. Then when I told her that we live here now, she wouldn't say another word."

"She sounds weird," Tim said, shaking his head.

"Tim!" his mother reproved.

Professor Harmon said seriously, "To me, Amy Goodwin sounds like a girl who has a problem."

18

"Well, I don't know about a problem," Sara replied with a sigh, "but she's sure not that friendly."

Professor Harmon leaned back in his chair and mused, "I've often found that when someone seems unfriendly and there is no reason why that person should be, it is because something is troubling him. If you follow the Christian principle of friendship, Sara, and take the first step in being friendly, you may be able to help Amy out of her troubles and at the same time gain a friend."

"But I have no idea what's troubling her," Sara replied with a puzzled shake of her head.

Tim spoke up, "I think I know who may."

"Who?" asked Sara eagerly.

"Vickie," Tim replied. "The Rabers were the Goodwin's nearest neighbors. If anybody'd know what's troubling Amy, Vickie would."

Sara's eyes brightened at the suggestion. "That's a neat idea, Tim. Would you ask her for me?"

Tim shook his head. "Uh-uh. Vickie would tell you more about Amy if you asked her yourself. Girls don't talk much about other girls in front of guys. Not as much as they would to another girl."

"You sure know all about women," Sam chimed in, grinning his crooked grin at his brother.

"That's only using good psychology, little brother," Tim grinned back.

"I think Tim's idea is a good one," their mother agreed.

"I was going to stop at Fox Ridge Farm tomorrow on the way home from school," Sara said thoughtfully. "I promised Vickie I'd exercise Dusty."

"Well, that's a swell time to ask her," Tim declared.

Mother stood up and started carrying dishes over to the sink. Sara and the boys helped her load them into the

19

dishwasher, then they headed for the television set.

"Don't you three have homework?" Dad called after them.

Tim stopped in midstride. "Homework?" he asked, blinking his eyes with surprise. "On the first day of school, Dad? You got to be kidding!"

Remembering what her father had said about Christian friendship, Sara tried her best to be friendly with Amy Goodwin the next day. But the strange girl seemed more quiet and illusive than ever. As Dad said, it was as if Amy really did have a problem and couldn't think of anything else.

Several times when Amy was called on in class, she wasn't listening and fumbled with the wrong answers. In social studies Mrs. Bailey had to repeat a question twice, and then Amy gave another wrong answer.

Alison Heston and her friends looked at Amy and then at one another, raising their eyebrows and rolling their eyes with superior smiles. Sara could tell by their gestures what they thought of Amy Goodwin.

"Stop by my desk on the way out," Mrs. Bailey told Amy when the buzzer sounded for dismissal.

Sara was one of the last to leave the room and when she passed the teacher's desk, she overheard Mrs. Bailey saying in a concerned voice, "What's the matter, Amy? I was looking over your record last year, and you were an "A" student in social studies. But now suddenly . . . ."

Sara couldn't hear any more for she had reached the hallway, and the din drowned out the teacher's words. Well, Dad's not the only one who thinks Amy has a problem, Sara told herself as she made her way to the cafeteria.

After school Sara got off the bus with Vickie and Huy.

They walked under the wooden arch above the entrance of the driveway which announced the horse farm in large black letters: FOX RIDGE FARM. AMERICAN SADDLE-BREDS. Ahead of them was a long lane which led to the stable. Sara's heart skipped a beat, as it always did, when she saw the big thoroughbred stallions in the corral next to the stable.

Today Mike Doney, Mr. Raber's new horse trainer, was putting Black Cloud, a handsome American Saddlebred, through his gaits. Mike was a small, wiry-looking man who rode with ease, as if he were part of his mount. Maybe that's because he had once been a jockey, Sara thought as she watched with admiration at the way Mike was trotting the beautiful black stallion. Huy went on to the stable to do his chores, and Sara followed Vickie up to the house.

"I got my jeans and boots in my gym bag," she informed the older girl.

"Okay, you can change in the powder room while I get into mine. Be down in a minute."

When Vickie returned, she looked as stunning in jeans and a plaid shirt as she did in a skirt and frilly blouse. Sara envied the girl's tall, slim shape, her startling blue eyes, and the long blond hair that bounced on her shoulders when she walked. Yet Vickie wasn't enamored with herself as some pretty girls might be. She seemed to be completely unaware of her good looks, as if they mattered not at all. It was easy to understand why Tim liked her so much.

"You don't know how grateful I am that you're willing to exercise Dusty," Vickie told Sara as she led the way to the stable. "That gives me more time with Blaze."

Blaze was Vickie's horse, a brown mare with a white star between her eyes. That summer while Vickie was in Nebraska, Sam had exercised Blaze while Sara had exercised

Dusty, a gentle gray mare whom she grew to love.

"I really should be the grateful one," Sara returned, laughing. "You know how much I like to ride Dusty."

The girls stopped at the tack room for the saddles, saddle blankets, and bridles. Huy, who had been mucking out the stalls, helped them tack up. Dusty nuzzled Sara with her velvety nose as the girl eased the bridle over the mare's head. Making sure the cinch strap was well fastened, Sara mounted. With a soft nudge of her knees against the mare's sides, she walked Dusty out the back door of the stable.

Vickie followed. They rode up a trail behind the stable that led across the top of an open field, jogging then loping their mounts. The wind rushed against Sara's cheeks, and a thrill of joy raced through her as it always did when she was in the saddle. She brought Dusty to an easy walking stride when they approached the woods that led to the marsh pond which separated their land from the Rabers.

"Let's ride back to the cabin," Vickie suggested.

They followed the old woods road through the tall ferns and low bushes. Even though it was early September, some of the maples were already beginning to turn a pretty pale yellow, and the Virginia creeper entwining the trunks was a flaming red. A soft wind hummed through the pines, sounding a little mournful with the end of summer.

They rode out of the woods into a small clearing. In the middle of the clearing was the cabin, its large stone chimney rising up along one side of it, as if to prop up the sagging logs.

The cabin looked just as it had when she had first seen it, Sara thought. Rusty pine needles were blown across the little wooden porch and several shakes were missing from the roof. It looked as deserted as ever, and as she stared at the old building, Sara thought back to the time when Huy Chau had run away from his sponsors in Philadelphia and had hidden there so that he could be close to his little brother, Dzung, who lived with a foster family in Maplewood. Of course everything had turned out all right. Mr. Raber had offered Huy a foster home at Fox Ridge Farm, and now Huy could be with his little brother any time he wanted.

They dismounted, and letting the horses graze in the clearing, the girls walked over to the cabin and sat on the sagging steps in the sun.

"I love it back here," Vickie said dreamily. "It's so quiet and away from everything. I used to ride here when I was a little girl and was troubled about something. See that big tree stump over there?" She pointed to an old lichen-covered stump along the edge of the clearing. "Well, that used to be my altar where I'd come to talk to God about my problems, and I still come here to pray. I never feel so close

Sara remembered when Huy Chau had hidden in the deserted cabin to be near his little brother, Dzung.

to God anywhere else as I do here."

She glanced over at Sara. "I think everyone needs a quiet place to be alone in, don't you?"

Sara nodded, puzzled that a girl like Vickie Raber should have problems and the need to be alone. But then, she thought, maybe even popular girls feel troubled and insecure at times.

They sat for a moment in silence, then Sara decided it was time to bring up the subject of Amy.

"I met Amy Goodwin yesterday in school," she began.

"She used to live in your house," Vickie said. "Do you know that?"

Sara nodded. "She told me."

Vickie reached down for a long brown pine needle and twirled it between her fingers. "Poor Amy. She has her problems."

"That's what I wanted to ask about," Sara said, her eyes bright with interest. "Tim told me you'd know what is troubling her because you were neighbors before her family moved out of the old Goodwin place."

At the mention of Tim's name, Vickie's cheeks grew a slight pink. Quickly recovering her composure she explained, "Ever since John Goodwin—that's Amy's father—lost his job at the iron works in town, things have gone downhill for the Goodwins."

Sara looked at the older girl inquiringly. "But they had the farm to fall back on, didn't they?"

Vickie shook her head. "There wasn't much of a living on the old Goodwin place. To make a success out of farming these days, you have to have expensive equipment and a lot of acres to plant and use as pasture. That's why John Goodwin had to work in town. Dad says he's a good mechanic, but the iron works had to lay off a lot of their employees, and John was one of the unfortunates."

Vickie paused with a sigh. "Then to add to their trouble, Amy's mother got seriously ill, and to pay all the medical bills, John had to sell the Goodwin place. Now we hear that Mrs. Goodwin is back in the hospital again. Anyway, they are renting a little house in Maplewood, and John is still unemployed. Dad said he heard that he has been spending a lot of his time at a local bar, drinking."

Sara didn't reply for a long moment. When she did, she murmured, "I guess when some people have as much trouble as John Goodwin, they try to drink their troubles away. It would be so much better to turn to God."

"I know," Vickie replied, shaking her head sadly, "but the Goodwins don't go to church." She tossed the pine needle away and added, "Amy used to be a smart kid, and she got along well with the kids in school and everything. But now, with all the trouble her family has had, she kind of gave up, like her father. Amy's not like some kids who can cover up their problems by being aggressive and putting on a good act. She's always been rather shy, and now, I hear, she's really gone into her shell."

"I know. She's not too friendly," Sara admitted. "The only thing she talked to me about was the old Goodwin place. But when I told her my family and I live there now, she wouldn't say anything more. It was almost as though she resented our being there."

"That's another thing," Vickie explained. "Amy loved the farm. Before he lost his job, her father bought her a horse from our stable so that she could ride all around the place. Amy loved that horse and it almost broke her heart when John had to sell Bumper back to us. Dad promised Amy that he'd never sell the horse to anyone else, that he'd always keep Bumper for her. But it wasn't the same for Amy. When

25

you love a horse as much as she loves Bumper, you want to know that she's all yours and nobody else's."

"I know," replied Sara. A lover of horses herself, she could understand the feeling. She took in a long breath and shook her head. "I wish I could get Amy to like me. Then maybe I could help her."

Vickie smiled and reached over to pat Sara's hand. "You're an okay kid, Sara." She looked across the clearing at the horses for a long moment through half-closed eyes. Then she sat up straight as if struck by a sudden thought. "I have an idea, Sara. Maybe there is a way we both can help Amy."

"How?" Sara was so excited she almost slid off the slanting step.

"You remember I mentioned Bumper, Amy's horse?" Vickie reminded her.

Sara nodded intently.

"Well, like every other horse we have, Bumper needs exercise. She's starting to get fat and that's not good. Mike and Dad have their hands full exercising the Saddlebreds, and now that school's started, Huy and I don't have all that time to exercise the other horses. Maybe if I ask Amy to help us with Bumper a couple times a week, she would."

"Oh, that would be neat!" Sara exclaimed. "Then when I come over to exercise Dusty, we could ride together."

"That's what I was thinking," Vickie said, a gleam in her blue eyes. "There's no better way to foster good friendship than to share a love for horses."

She got up from the step and brushed the pine needles off her jeans. "Tell you what, Sara. I'll ask Amy in school tomorrow. What time does the ninth grade eat lunch?"

"The fourth period," Sara replied.

"Oh, good. That's my free period. I'll get a pass to the cafeteria and ask Amy then."

3

Partners

How would you like a project in American history to work on?" Mrs. Bailey asked her social studies class the next day. A groan went up. Mrs. Bailey looked at the class, and smiling faintly, shook her head. "I'm glad to hear you're all so enthusiastic."

Another protest, much louder this time, made Mrs. Bailey rap on her desk for attention. "Wait until I explain before you moan and groan," she told them. "This isn't a project your teacher thought up. It's a community project, presented by the Maplewood Historical Society for our ninth-grade social studies classes."

"What's the project about?" a boy in the back of the room called out in a skeptical voice.

"Raise your hand, Jason, when you have a question," Mrs. Bailey reminded him.

In answer to the question, she replied, "The Maplewood Historical Society is putting together a book about colonial Maplewood and would like us to help them by unearthing some original facts about our town. We all know that Maplewood is an old colonial town, just seeping with history."

Sara smiled to herself. Mrs. Bailey loved to use colorful verbs, like "seeping," when she was trying to interest the class in something. And right now she was doing her best to interest them in the American history project.

"What the Historical Society wants you young people to do is to look around your town for original ideas to write about," Mrs. Bailey went on, her eyes sparkling with lively enthusiasm. "You're not to go to the library and just copy material from one of our local history books, although I have asked Miss Finney at the public library to reserve those books which you may use as background material for the persons or things you have chosen to write about. But what the Historical Society really wants you to do is original research. Be detectives," Mrs. Bailey continued. "Interview some of our older people who remember things their grandparents have told them. Search for old letters and diaries. Snoop around unlikely places to dig out clues that will lead you to the subject matter you are working on. When you have researched your topics thoroughly, write an essay about your findings. And, if possible, you may bring in old letters, diaries, or other memorabilia to illustrate your essays. There will be prizes of $50 for the best essay, $25 for the second best, and $15 for the third best."

A soft whistle came from the back of the room. Mrs. Bailey was making the project sound attractive, and the entire class was beginning to share her enthusiasm. A slim arm waved from the center of the room.

"Yes, Alison?" Mrs. Bailey asked.

The tall attractive girl stood up and asked, "May we work together as partners?"

The teacher nodded. "Yes, if you're willing to get the same grade as your partner and share the prize money if you should win."

"Oh, good!" Alison said, sliding down into her seat, and for a few minutes the class was buzzing with students leaning over their desks and choosing their best friends for partners. Alison was gesturing to a blond girl named Tracy, pointing to Tracy and then to herself, which told anybody who was watching her that she was choosing Tracy Wiggen as her partner. Tracy nodded with satisfaction and beamed a smile back at Alison.

When Mrs. Bailey waved for order, it seemed that everyone in class had a partner except Amy Goodwin and Sara. Sara sighed and glanced wistfully at her desk. If she were at her old school in Philadelphia, she and her best friend, Beth Andrews, would be partners. It was difficult—no, terrible—being a newcomer, Sara thought, fighting back the resentment that was welling up inside her. She had no idea that being the new girl in class would be so hard.

She picked up a pencil and started to doodle on her tablet. It was a habit she had whenever anything bothered her. She'd doodle curlicues and pictures all over the place.

Well, she thought, doodling a particularly large swirl, she'd just have to write her essay alone. But what did she know about the history of Maplewood? Being here only one summer wasn't like living here all her life. How could she possibly find anything to write about? Her essay would be a flop. She just knew it would be.

She was still in a dark mood when she walked into the

cafeteria during fourth period. She didn't feel very hungry, so she took only a bowl of soup and an apple. She was about to take her tray to the table in the back where Amy was sitting, then changed her mind. If anyone needed Dad's Christian friendship today, it was she, Sara, she told herself. She decided she would eat alone. Being seen with Amy Goodwin wouldn't help her social status, which was nearing rock bottom already.

She found an empty place at the end of a table and sat down. She didn't look up at anybody but concentrated on eating her soup. So it was with surprise that she heard a voice across the table say, "Hey, you're in my homeroom. You're new around here, aren't you?"

That was the last thing Sara wanted to be reminded of, and she glared at the smiling blond boy sitting across from her. Then, to her surprise, she felt her face begin to burn. She twitched uncomfortably in her seat. She never blushed like that when meeting a strange boy before. She nodded and looked quickly away.

"I'm Doug Cooper," the boy went on. He waited for her to say something, but the words wouldn't come. Finally he arose and picked up his empty tray. "See ya around," he said, giving her a brief nod as he left the table.

"How stupid can you get?" Sara scolded herself after he had left. "Here was a good-looking guy who wanted to be friendly and you all but ignored him!"

Sara nibbled miserably at her apple, her eyes downcast on her empty soup bowl. She was so absorbed with her dismal thoughts that she didn't notice Vickie Raber entering the rear door of the cafeteria. It wasn't until a few minutes later when Vickie's hand rested on her shoulder that she looked up with surprise.

"Hi," Vickie said cheerfully. "I thought you might like to

30

know that I asked Amy if she'd exercise Bumper after school, and she said she would." Vickie turned quickly toward the door. "Got to run now. See you later."

"Oh—uh, okay," Sara called after her.

In her morbid preoccupation with herself, Sara had completely forgotten about her plans with Amy that afternoon. She glanced back at the girl eating alone, and suddenly she felt worse than ever. How could she have been so unfeeling, thinking only about her own petty problems and forgetting about Amy's much larger ones?"

I'll make it up to her after school, Sara vowed. I'll try to be friends with Amy Goodwin. I really will!

The afternoon classes seemed to last forever, but finally Sara found herself getting off the school bus with Vickie and Huy. She was in Dusty's stall, tacking up, when Amy arrived at the stable on her bicycle.

Sara watched the girl walk slowly up to Bumper's stall and stand there looking at the horse. Thinking that no one else was around, Amy opened the stall door and threw her arms around the neck of the chestnut mare.

Sara couldn't remain silent any longer. Remembering her vow to make friends with Amy, she called from the next stall, "Hi, Amy. I'll help you tack up if you want me to."

Amy stepped back with surprise at seeing Sara. "What are you doing here?" she asked.

"Tacking up Dusty," Sara replied simply. "I like to ride, too."

As Sara followed Amy to the tack room, she asked, "How did Bumper get her name?"

Amy smiled one of her rare smiles. "It was when I rode her for the first time and I kept bumping up and down in the saddle. I told everyone that she sure was bumpy. After that we all called her Bumper."

31

Sara giggled, then added hastily, "Bet you can ride her okay now."

"I've learned to put her through her gaits," Amy replied modestly.

They carried the tack back to Bumper's stall. As they were saddling the horse, Sara said, "I know a neat trail around the marsh pond."

Amy looked up with interest, "You do? I never knew there was a trail there."

"There wasn't when you lived there," Sara said. "It was made just this summer." She threw the stirrup over the saddle horn so that Amy could draw up the cinch to the third hole in the heavy strap. "Would you like to ride it?"

Amy fastened the cinch then looked up, her eyes bright with curiosity. "Sure. Lead the way."

Sara's spirits rose as they jogged across the field together. Amy was like a different girl. The farther they rode, the more relaxed she became, and by the time they were walking their horses down the woods road, both girls were chattering together like old friends. *Vickie sure was right*, Sara thought, smiling to herself. There was no better way to foster good friendship than to share a love for horses.

They turned off the woods road onto a narrow trail and followed the blaze marks through the woods to the Harmon side of the pond. They paused by a large beech tree to let the horses drink at a spring that bubbled out of the ground between the thick roots. Above the spring the trail led upward until it came out to a field on the Harmon property which Sara had named Green Meadow.

In a corner of the field, sheltered by a grove of hemlocks, was the shed which Dad and her brothers had transformed into an art studio that summer for Mom. They had even built a skylight in the roof.

"I wonder if Mom's painting," Sara said as they dismounted by the door of the shed.

"Is your mother an artist?" asked Amy.

Sara nodded proudly and knocked on the door. When there was no answer, she opened it and they peeked inside. The studio was empty.

"Come in and I'll show you some of Mom's canvases," Sara invited, stepping aside so that the other girl could enter the studio.

Amy's eyes widened as she glanced around the room. "Oh my! I don't remember the old shed looking like this before."

An artist's easel dominated the center, directly underneath the skylight. On a rough board table underneath the back loft were paints, many jars and bottles, and a stack of unused canvases. The walls, which had been left their original weathered boards, were covered with bright and colorful paintings. Most of them were landscapes of the old Goodwin place which Amy knew so well.

"There's a picture of the woods," she exclaimed as she walked around the room, looking at all the canvases. "And the pond. And—and the barn!"

"Do you know what this one is?" Sara asked, pointing to the painting on her mother's easel.

"Why, it's our house!" Amy cried, staring at the painting of the old stone house that had once been her home. She flushed and the muscles about her mouth tightened. "I—I mean it's *your* house now."

She stood looking at the painting for a long moment, then crumpled down on a stool by the easel, her eyes shining with sudden tears.

"Oh, Amy," Sara said in distress. "I didn't mean to make you feel this way."

"I know you didn't," Amy replied in a choked voice. Then, sniffling back her tears, she let everything out.

"I—I cried buckets when Daddy said we'd have to move from here. But Mama needed that operation or she would have died, and Daddy had just lost his job and...."

Sara sank down beside her. At that moment she didn't care what Alison Heston or her friends thought about Amy. Sara liked this troubled girl and wanted her as a friend.

She put her arm around Amy's drooped shoulders and in the awkward silence that followed, she looked up at her mother's painting. As she studied the brushstrokes of the old stone house, her troubled face lighted up with a smile at the birth of a brilliant idea. Why hadn't she thought about that before?

Breathlessly she asked, "Amy, have you thought what you're going to write about for the American history project?"

The girl wiped her watery eyes on the sleeve of her shirt and looked surprised at Sara's sudden change of subject.

"No. Why?"

"Well, I've just had a terrific inspiration, if you want me as a partner," Sara went on excitedly.

Amy still looked baffled. "Sure, I'd like you for a partner, Sara, but what's your idea?"

Sara pointed to the painting. "You said an ancestor of yours built the house in 1768. He would certainly fit into colonial Maplewood."

A look of understanding flashed across Amy's pale, narrow face. "I see what you mean, Sara. We could write about Adam Goodwin." She paused and her forehead puckered. "But I don't know anything about him. It was so long ago."

"Well, we could look at those local history books in the library. Maybe there's something about him in them."

"And we do have the old family Bible," Amy mused, warming up to the subject. "Maybe we can find some family history in that."

She hesitated, then looked at Sara, her eyes glowing. "I do know something about Adam Goodwin," she admitted. "Can you keep a secret, Sara?"

"Sure," Sara answered, with an excited giggle.

"Well, there's been a story in our family that Adam Goodwin hid a treasure at the old Goodwin place."

"Has anybody ever found it?" Sara broke in with lively interest.

Amy shook her head. "Daddy said he and his father searched the house and the barn several times but couldn't find anything. In fact, I guess all the generations of Goodwins have searched for Adam's treasure and never found it. But I just know it's here somewhere. I've always had that feeling, Sara."

Amy paused, and Sara caught the bright look on her face. "Maybe we could look for it together. If we found it, it would be something to write about in our essay."

"Oh, that'd be neat!" Sara exclaimed. "I'd love to help you hunt for it."

Sara glanced back at the painting of the old stone house and felt a tingle of excitement run through her. A treasure hidden at the old Goodwin place—their very own farm! Wouldn't it be something if they could find it for Amy's family and for their American history essay!

4

Another Kind of Hero

The next day in social studies class they announced their topics for the American history project. So many students wanted to write about Maplewood's most prominent landmark, the old gristmill on Main Street, that Mrs. Bailey had to suggest different topics for them.

Of course Alison Heston said that she and Tracy were doing their essay on Major Benjamin Heston, Alison's illustrious ancestor who had fought in the American Revolution and was a personal friend of General George Washington.

"Did George Washington sleep at your ancestral home?" one of the guys called out jokingly.

Alison tossed her head and gave him a flippant answer. "I'll see if I can find out in the major's diary."

"You are fortunate to have your ancestor's diary," Mrs. Bailey said with enthusiasm. "Diaries are excellent sources of firsthand information."

When Sara and Amy announced that they were writing their essay on Adam Goodwin, the teacher complimented them on their choice of an original subject. "I don't believe much has been written about Adam Goodwin," she told them, "but I did come across an interesting account about him in one of the local history books I had Miss Finney put on reserve."

On their way to the cafeteria after class, Amy said, with a hint of scorn in her voice, "I just knew Alison would write about her famous ancestor. Benjamin Heston was an officer in the American Revolution and was in all kinds of exciting battles. Everybody in Maplewood still looks upon him as the town hero. Compared to him, Adam Goodwin doesn't stand a chance."

"But Mrs. Bailey complimented us on the choice of an original subject, and she said there was an interesting account about Adam Goodwin in one of the history books in the library," Sara reminded her. "Maybe we can find something exciting about him, too."

"I don't know what." Amy shook her head, disheartened. "When I told Daddy about our American history project last night, he said that Adam Goodwin was a Quaker, and Quakers were, and still are, pacifists. You can imagine how popular pacifists were in Maplewood during the American Revolution."

"There's still the treasure," Sara responded cheerfully, determined not to give in to Amy's doubts. "It may prove interesting if we can find out what the treasure is and why Adam hid it at the old Goodwin place."

At the mention of the treasure, Amy brightened. "Do you

think that reference book Mrs. Bailey mentioned will have something in it about Adam's treasure?"

Sara grinned. "Could be. Let's go to the library after school and find out."

As soon as their last class was over, the girls hurried out of the school and walked the few blocks to the public library. Just before they came to the town square, they passed a large colonial mansion set back from the street by a long green lawn that was bordered by a wrought-iron fence. It was a graceful old stone house surrounded by tall elms, and it even had a porte-cochere where the driveway curved up to the front door.

"Oh, what a lovely old house," Sara said admiringly.

"Oh, what a lovely old house," Sara said admiringly. "I wonder who lives there."

"I wonder who lives there."

"That's the old Mansion House," Amy replied. "It used to be the ironmaster's mansion long ago when Major Heston built his iron furnace here in Maplewood. Back in those days it was called Heston Furnace, but now it's the Heston Iron Works, and Alison's father owns it. Anyway, she and her family live in the Mansion House."

"Wow, so this is where Alison lives!" Sara breathed as she paused to take another look at the beautiful old home.

When they arrived at the public library on the square, they stopped at the circulation desk to ask Miss Finney where the reserve shelf was with the books about colonial Maplewood.

"You're the first ones to ask about those books," the librarian told them as she led the way through the stacks to the far end of the library. "Nobody else is using them now, so they are all here."

Sara noticed that there were about a dozen old volumes stacked on the reserve shelf. When the librarian left them, Amy groaned, "I hope we won't have to go through every one of these books to find the one Mrs. Bailey referred to. Some of them are awfully thick."

"We don't have to go through the entire book," Sara told her. "We can look in the index for Adam Goodwin's name, and if it's not there, we can look for it in the section on the eighteenth century."

Amy took a deep breath. "Okay. You start at this end of the shelf and I'll begin at the other end."

Sara picked up her first book, a brown, dusty old volume, and paged through the index. She then scanned through the chapter telling about Maplewood during colonial days and the American Revolution, but there was no mention of Adam Goodwin. She chose the next book and was leafing through it when Amy exclaimed, "Hey, I found Adam's name in this index."

Sara peered over Amy's shoulder as she turned to the page, but they were disappointed to find that Adam Goodwin's name was mentioned only in a list of property owners in the township of Maplewood.

Amy shut the book and they resumed their search.

"There sure is a lot about Major Benjamin Heston in these books," Sara noted. "In this one he's called the hero of Maplewood, just as you said, Amy. The author writes that he was 'an ardent and fearless patriot.' Alison will have her work cut out for her, going through all this material."

Amy smiled thinly. "Well, that's the price she'll have to pay for having such a famous ancestor." She glanced ruefully at the shelf of books in front of her. "I wish we had asked Mrs. Bailey for the name of the book where she found that interesting account of Adam Goodwin."

"Knowing Mrs. Bailey, she wouldn't have told us," Sara answered. "She'd have said that finding the right book was part of the research."

"Yeah, I know," Amy said with a wry grin.

They went back to work again. For a long while neither girl spoke a word as she riffled through the musty old pages. Finally they were down to the last two books on the shelf. Sara took one and Amy the other.

"It has to be in one of these books," Amy said. "Let's take them over to that reading table."

They carried the books to the nearest table and sat down. Suddenly Sara was aware of Amy frantically turning pages. She looked up from her book. "Have you found something?"

Amy didn't answer right away, then she exclaimed, "There's a section here on residents living in and around

Maplewood during the American Revolution, and here's a whole page and a half about Adam Goodwin."

"Oh, good!" Sara said. "This must be the book Mrs. Bailey meant." She slammed her own book shut and leaned over Amy's so that she could read the account, too.

"The author writes that Adam Goodwin was a Quaker and attended the Friends Meeting here in Maplewood," Amy pointed out. She ran her finger down the page and when she spoke again, her voice rose with excitement.

"Look, Sara, what it says here. 'Adam Goodwin helped a wounded British officer, a Colonel Edwin Wilkes, by giving him shelter and caring for his wounds.'"

Sara's eyes scanned the page, then she caught her breath with surprise. "And it says that Adam Goodwin was imprisoned for helping an enemy officer!"

Amy moaned, "Oh, wow, that wouldn't have made him much of a hero in Maplewood."

"Maybe not in Maplewood at that time, but the author writes that he was a hero in another way. Look, Amy, he writes, 'Adam Goodwin upheld his religious principles by giving his life for them when he died in prison.'"

"So that's what happened to my ancestor," Amy said in a tight voice. "He died in prison."

"It also mentions his wife, Elizabeth, who was visiting her family in Philadelphia at that time," Sara went on reading. "Let's see—it was the fall of 1777. The time the British captured Philadelphia and defeated the Continental Army in the Battle of Germantown."

She turned the page quickly and read, "'Elizabeth and their son would have been safe in Philadelphia with her Quaker family, but Elizabeth came back to Maplewood to try to get her husband released from prison. However, with the British winning all the battles and occupying Philadelphia, tension in Maplewood was running high. Suspicion and hatred sprang up against all Quaker pacifists, and many of them were imprisoned. Major Heston, who had Adam Goodwin arrested, would not release him.' Then it goes on to say that 'Adam Goodwin was badly treated in prison and died a martyr's death.' "

Amy fixed her eyes on the page and said in an unbelieving tone, "Major Heston had Adam Goodwin imprisoned, and my ancestor died a martyr's death!" She sank back in her chair.

"Oh, wow, Sara, it'll be like turning up a hornet's nest when Alison reads about her ancestor and I read about mine. You know that Mrs. Bailey said we'd be reading our essays aloud in class."

"Well, it's good to bring together two different points of view," Sara pointed out. "Daddy says that's what history is all about. And you needn't be ashamed to read about your ancestor, Amy. He was just as much a hero as Alison's, and maybe more so because he died for his religious principles. Personally, I think that's more important than anything else."

Amy glanced at Sara with surprise, then a look of pride flashed across her face. "I don't know much about religion, but maybe you're right about Adam Goodwin. Maybe he was another kind of hero."

For the space of a moment or two Amy was silent. Then she bent over the book again. "There's one more paragraph, Sara. The author writes, 'During the hard winter of 1777, Elizabeth died of pneumonia, and Adam's parents moved to the farm to take care of their grandson, Lemuel. Lemuel grew up to become a prosperous farmer. When he died, he deeded the farm to his son, and through the years it has passed from one generation of Goodwins to another.' "

She stopped reading and let out a long breath. "That's the end of the account."

"Let's ask Miss Finney if we can photocopy these pages," Sara suggested. "Then we won't have to write them down. It'd save a lot of time."

Miss Finney showed them the copy machine and explained how to operate it. Sara emptied the coins from her purse and found that she had enough left from her lunch money to make copies for both Amy and herself.

"Don't forget to write down the name of the book and the author," Amy reminded her after the copying was done and they had returned to the reading table with their papers.

"The title is *Portraits of Prominent Citizens in Maplewood During the American Revolution*," Sara said as she scribbled down the title on her copy of the pages from the book. "And the author is George Matterson."

The girls had been so intent in reading about Adam Goodwin that they had completely lost track of the time. When Sara happened to glance up at the wall clock, she exclaimed, "Look what time it is! I must run or my family will be sending out a search party."

"Do you think you can come to my house tomorrow after school and look at our family Bible?" Amy asked as they hurried out of the library. "Maybe we can find out some more about Adam Goodwin."

"I'd love to," Sara replied. "I'll ride my bike to school tomorrow so that I won't have to walk home."

As they strolled up the street together, they talked about what they had read in the library and how they would write their essay.

"We'll emphasize Adam's pacifism and why he was justified in helping a wounded enemy soldier," Sara suggested. "We can end with Adam's dying a martyr's death in prison which proved him to be another kind of hero."

Amy had been listening in silence, but now a thought struck her.

"That's what we can call our essay, Sara," she exclaimed, her face lighting up. " 'Another Kind of Hero.' I like the sound of that, don't you?"

Sara nodded with enthusiasm and smiled at her friend. "That's a neat title, Amy, and we'll have an exciting enough subject to write about. Our essay will be original, too. I have the feeling that nobody has written about pacifism, or the Quaker point of view, in Maplewood's colonial history before."

"Not with Major Heston always being the town hero," Amy agreed with a wry twist of her mouth.

They had chattered on so intently about their essay that before they realized it, Amy had walked Sara halfway home. It was the red Chevette that sped by them in the direction of town that broke their concentration.

"Wow, somebody's in a hurry," Sara said.

"That was Pete Simmons," Amy told her, "and did you see who was with him?"

Sara nodded. "Alison Heston."

She wouldn't have thought anything about Alison riding down the road in a red Chevette with an older boy if Amy hadn't said, with a puzzled frown, "Pete has football practice every day after school, and Alison's going out for cheerleading and should be in the gym practicing. I wonder what they are doing speeding down this road this time of day."

Sara turned around and squinted after the passing car. Knowing how much cheerleading must mean to a girl like Alison, she was beginning to wonder, too.

5
Shadows in the Night

Sara went home with Amy the next day after school. The Goodwins lived in a row house on a crowded street three blocks from Maplewood High.

"You sure don't have far to walk to school," Sara said as she followed Amy up the front steps onto a small stoop. Amy unlocked the front door and ushered the way into a small, untidy living room that was cluttered with newspapers and items of clothing lying around.

"It's hard to keep things picked up with Mama in the hospital," Amy apologized as she swooped up a stray sock on one of the chairs and an old jacket that had been draped over the sofa.

"Daddy goes in to Philadelphia to see her almost every

day, and sometimes he doesn't get home until dinnertime," she added.

"How is your mother?" Sara asked with concern.

"Oh, she's getting along okay," Amy replied. "But it will be a while before she can leave the hospital, and then after she does get home, she has to be real careful. It's good Daddy and I can both cook, but we're not that great at keeping things tidy."

She steered Sara across the living room to an even smaller room where a large oval table took up most of the space. "I'm glad you could come home with me after school to see the Bible, Sara. I looked through it last night and found some interesting things. Let's sit here at the dining room table and I'll show you."

Pushing aside an empty coffee cup and a plate with a half-eaten doughnut on it, Amy opened a thick, ancient-looking book with a black embossed cover. Turning to a page in front of the Bible, she showed Sara the family genealogy.

Sara noticed Adam Goodwin's name written at the top of the family tree in a beautiful flowing scroll. Next to his name his wife, Elizabeth, had written hers. And below their two names was Lemuel's. The names of all their descendants followed. Amy's name was the last one on the page.

"Daddy wrote my name there the day I was born," Amy said proudly. There was a sparkle of lively interest in her brown eyes as she pulled out a long sheet of yellow, wrinkled paper that had been tucked between the next two pages. She unfolded the paper reverently, as if it were a fragile, precious thing.

"I found this while I was looking through the Bible last night," she chimed triumphantly. "Read it, Sara."

Sara bent over the paper. It was written in a spidery hand

46

and hard to read, but slowly she made out the words and began to read them aloud.

" 'This is an account that my father told me concerning my grandfather, Adam Goodwin.' "

Amy interrupted and explained, "It's written by Lemuel's son and Adam's grandson."

Sara nodded and peered down at the name Levi Goodwin at the bottom of the paper. Then, tracing the wavering script with her finger, she continued reading.

" 'During the first week of October, 1777, after the Battle of Germantown, a British officer and a gentleman by the name of Colonel Edwin Wilkes came to my grandfather's farmhouse seeking shelter. My grandmother was visiting her family in Philadelphia at the time, so she did not know the details. But a Friend from the Meeting told her what had happened here while she was away.

" 'Colonel Edwin Wilkes had been wounded during the battle at Germantown and got separated from his men in the heavy fog that hung over Germantown that day. It seems that in the fog he lost his direction and traveled north instead of south to Philadelphia, where he had hoped to join his troops. After walking three days, he stumbled into our farmyard. He was near death when my grandfather found him lying outside the barn. Grandfather took him in, bound his wounds, and nursed him back to health, hiding him all this time from the Continental Army.

" 'When he recovered and was well enough to travel, the colonel left my grandfather's farm. He must have been seen leaving because the local militia was warned, and that same day Major Benjamin Heston and four men rode out to the farm and arrested Grandfather. Shortly after the arrest, my grandmother and my father, Lemuel, then a babe in arms, returned from Philadelphia. Adam's parents came to live with them. Grandmother and several Friends from the Meeting pleaded with Major Heston to release Adam from prison, but the major had branded Adam a traitor and wouldn't even let my grandmother or the Friends visit him. Thus Adam Goodwin remained in prison until he died.' "

Sara looked up with shining eyes. "Levi's account is just like the one we read about in the library, only it's much more detailed. This is great, Amy!"

Amy nodded and added, "It seems so real, too, written by his grandson."

Sara bent over the paper again and finished reading, " 'Many Friends here in Maplewood were mistreated during the Revolution, and feeling toward us is still bitter. But my father will not leave the farm. He told me that this was the house Adam Goodwin built, and he intended to stay here in respect for his father, who upheld our religious principles that all men are children of God and that it is our duty to help friend and foe alike when suffering from the persecution of war.

> Levi Goodwin,
> Grandson of Adam Goodwin' "

Sara stopped reading and for a moment the two girls were silent. Then Sara said, "That last paragraph is a beautiful tribute to your ancestor. We'll certainly use it in our essay."

"I thought you'd be interested in Levi's account," Amy said proudly. Then with a sigh she added, "Neither it nor the book in the library mentions the treasure, though."

Seeing her friend's disappointment, Sara said softly, "I think the best treasure Adam left his family was his Christian charity toward an enemy. It's like the parable Jesus told of the Good Samaritan."

"I know that story," Amy said. "Mama read it to me when I was a little girl." She took the yellowed, wrinkled paper that Sara handed back to her and put it carefully into the Bible again.

As Sara watched her, she said, "Even though Levi didn't mention anything about his grandfather's treasure, I don't think we should give up on it. We haven't even started looking for it yet."

She paused as if struck by a sudden thought. "Amy, why can't we start hunting for it right now! It's Friday and we'll have all day tomorrow to search. Do you think your father would let you spend the weekend with us?"

Amy brightened. "Daddy won't be back until late, but I know he won't mind as long as he knows where I am. What about your parents?"

"Oh, they won't mind," Sara replied. "They'll be happy to have you."

"Okay, then I'll leave Daddy a note in the kitchen."

Sara helped Amy word the note to her father so that Mr. Goodwin wouldn't worry, then Amy packed a few things in her gym bag and got her bike out of the garage. Together the girls pedaled up the road to Marsh Pond Farm, Amy's gym bag swaying back and forth on her handlebars.

Just as Sara had predicted, her parents were happy to have Amy spend the weekend with them, and so was Tim. Even Sam, who never showed much interest in the friends Sara brought home, was all smiles when he was introduced to Amy.

During dinner everybody listened intently while the girls told about their American history project. Professor Harmon, who taught history at Maplewood College, was especially interested in Adam Goodwin. Only Sam looked a bit downcast.

After the girls finished talking, he admitted, "I was going to write about Adam Goodwin for my American history essay."

"Have you started your research yet?" asked his father.

Sam shook his head.

"Well, since the girls have already begun theirs, I suggest you choose another topic. Besides, I think it is fitting that Amy writes about Adam Goodwin since he is her ancestor."

Sam looked across the table at Amy and a smile quirked one corner of his mouth. "Yeah, you're right, Dad. I'll think up another topic. Maybe I can dig up some colonial science around Maplewood. Could be Ben Franklin visited here and did one of his experiments."

"I know one thing you better not write about," warned Tim.

"What's that?" asked Sam.

"Computers," replied Tim with a teasing twinkle. "I don't think they had them in Maplewood in colonial days."

After they helped Mom clear the table, Sara took Amy to her room, and the girls discussed where they would search for the treasure.

"Adam probably hid it in this house," Amy suggested.

"It would be helpful if we could imagine the house as it was when he lived here," Sara said. "I'm sure there have been a lot of changes made since then."

"Your family sure made some nice changes," Amy said, glancing around the room at the soft-colored rose walls and frilly curtains that hung at the bay window. "This used to be my bedroom, too."

"It *was?*" cried Sara. "Did you choose it because of the bay window?"

Amy nodded. "I liked to sit on the window seat and read."

"That's exactly what I like to do," Sara said. "Oh, Amy, we do have a lot in common!"

Amy laughed, and Sara thought how different Amy was now that she had a friend. *And how different I am, too,* Sara told herself soberly.

Aloud she said, "Getting back to the treasure, do you think Adam's imprisonment could have had anything to do with his hiding it?"

"What do you mean?" Amy asked, puzzled.

"Well, I thought that if Adam hid something valuable, it would be logical that he hid it before he went off to prison. Maybe he thought that Elizabeth, his wife, would not come back to Maplewood, or that the army would occupy the house. I've read about how people during the Revolution hid their valuables when they had to leave their houses in a hurry."

Amy nodded thoughtfully. "Yes, that's true, but Elizabeth did come back."

"But when Adam was dragged off to prison, he had no way of knowing that," Sara said.

Amy sat for a moment, turning the idea over in her head. Then swinging around on the window seat, she gathered up her copied pages from *Portraits of Prominent Citizens in Maplewood During the American Revolution* and said, "Let's show this to Sam. Since he's interested in Adam Goodwin, too, he may have some ideas."

Sara hesitated. "You don't mind telling my family about the treasure?"

"Of course not," Amy replied. "After all they're living here now, and it wouldn't be right to search through the house without letting them know."

"Well, all right," Sara said. "I know they'll keep it a secret."

The girls found Sam studying in his room across the hall.

"Stumped or something?" he asked when Sara popped her head through the door.

"How did you know?" she asked.

"Oh, I got ESP," Sam teased. "You might as well come in. Maybe I can help."

The girls settled themselves on the edge of Sam's bed, and Amy showed him the account of Adam Goodwin. After Sam read it, he gave a low whistle through his teeth and said, "This sure will make an original subject for the American history project. I wonder how many people in Maplewood besides Mrs. Bailey know this story?"

"My family does because of Levi's account in the family Bible," Amy said, "but I don't believe many other people know about it."

"What we wonder," put in Sara, "is if Adam's imprisonment could have anything to do with his hiding a treasure here."

Sam's eyes popped wide open. "You mean there's a treasure hidden here too?"

"There's been talk in our family that Adam Goodwin hid a treasure here at the old Goodwin place," Amy explained. "But nobody's been able to find it. Daddy searched the house for it with his father, as I guess every generation of Goodwins have done. But they never found the treasure."

Sam held their gaze, his hazel eyes sparkling with interest. "Wow, if you girls find that treasure, you'll really have something to write about."

"Promise you won't say a word in school about the treasure—not even to Kenny," Sara warned. "If word got out in school that Adam Goodwin hid a treasure at the old Goodwin place, we could have plenty of treasure seekers around."

Sam gave them a tilted grin. "I'll keep mum if you'll let me help hunt for it."

"Is that blackmail or a bribe?" Sara asked, laughing.

"Call it whatever you like, Twinny. Is it a deal?"

Sara turned to Amy. "Should we let him, partner?"

Amy laughed at the twins' good-natured bantering and nodded.

"I'm glad you agree," Sara replied, "because Sam's the brain of the family. Okay, Sam, you're in."

Sam got right down to business. "You said you wondered if Adam's imprisonment could have anything to do with his hiding a treasure. Why is that so important?"

"I thought it may help us find the treasure," Sara

Not one shadow but two moved stealthily toward the barn.

explained. "Like where would Adam Goodwin hide something valuable if he knew he was to be imprisoned and was in a hurry to hide it."

Sam blinked thoughtfully. "I see what you mean." He ran his fingers through his thatch of unruly hair. "Wouldn't Adam have let his wife know where he hid it before he was dragged off to prison?"

"How could he if Elizabeth wasn't here when Major Heston arrested him?" asked Sara. "And Levi Goodwin wrote that the major wouldn't let her or anybody else visit Adam in prison."

"But Adam must have let somebody in the family know that he hid a treasure, if his descendants knew about it and have been looking for it all these years," Sam reasoned. "Maybe he left Elizabeth a note."

"That's it!" exclaimed Sara. "He must have. And before she died, Elizabeth must have told Adam's parents about the treasure."

Amy shook her head thoughtfully. "But if Adam did leave Elizabeth a note, it was never found."

Sam got up from his desk and walked over to the window. "Boy, Mrs. Bailey was right when she said we have to be detectives. Researching the past is like solving a mystery."

"Like where did Adam Goodwin hide his treasure," Amy added with a sigh.

Sam turned to the window to look out into the night. The trees by the pond and the dark shape of the barn stood out like silhouettes in the moonlight. The night was so bright that the barn and house cast long shadows across the yard.

Sam stared at the driveway, a silvery swathe in the moonlight. Suddenly he stiffened. Out of the semidarkness, he glimpsed a moving shadow. Not one shadow but two, moving stealthily down the driveway toward the barn.

He swung around to face the girls. "I think I just got a glimpse of our first treasure seekers," he told them.

"What are you talking about?" asked Sara.

Sam gestured to the window. "Take a look for yourselves."

He switched off the light so that they could see better. Sara drew in her breath as she saw the two shadows move about the barn.

With Amy trembling by their side, the twins stood transfixed while they watched the shadows meet and melt into one as they disappeared through the dark doorway of the barn.

6

Discovery in the Secretary

Sam flung open his closet door and grabbed a jacket off the hook.

"What are you going to do?" Sara asked.

"Find out who's prowling around inside our barn this time of night," he said, reaching across his desk for his pocket flashlight.

"Wait, we'll come with you," Sara said. "But don't you think we ought to tell Dad or Tim?"

"By the time we explained everything to them, whoever is out there may be gone," Sam replied.

The girls grabbed sweaters and followed Sam down the back stairs. The kitchen was dark, but they could hear a TV concert blaring from the living room. They were about to let

56

themselves out the side door when suddenly a voice behind them called out sharply, "Who's there?"

They swung around at the sound of their mother's voice. Mrs. Harmon reached over to the wall switch, and the kitchen light blazed on.

"Sam—Sara! Where are you going this time of night?"

They retreated from the door and came back into the kitchen. Sam stood, arms akimbo, as his mother held her gaze on them. "Oh, Mom! There goes our element of surprise."

"Whatever are you talking about?" Mrs. Harmon asked.

"We saw two shadows out by the barn," explained Sara, "and we think somebody's out there prowling around."

A look of concern flashed across Mrs. Harmon's face. "I believe this is a matter for your father and Tim," she said, turning and hurrying back toward the living room.

By the time Professor Harmon and Tim listened to their story and got their jackets on, Sam grumbled that it would be too late to catch the prowlers. But he led the way to the barn anyway.

Sara felt left out that her father had insisted that she and Amy stay in the kitchen with Mom. It seemed like hours had gone by until Dad and the boys returned.

"What did you find out?" Mom asked nervously.

Professor Harmon shook his head. "We didn't see or hear a thing. The old barn was as dark and as quiet as a tomb." He looked soberly at the twins and Amy. "Are you sure you saw someone out there?"

"For the tenth time, Dad, we're sure," replied Sam.

"We saw two shadowy figures go into the barn," Sara added firmly.

Amy nodded agreement.

"Well, whoever it was either left before we got there or

found a good hiding place," Tim spoke up.

"I knew they'd beat it when they saw the side porch light go on and heard the three of us charging across the yard," Sam grumbled. "Anyway, first thing tomorrow morning I'm going out there to look around again."

"To look for what?" asked Tim.

Sam shrugged. "Who knows. Maybe the prowlers left something behind that could be a clue."

Professor and Mrs. Harmon returned to their TV concert in the living room while the young people raided the refrigerator. After their search in the barn, Tim declared he was starved. He made himself a Dagwood sandwich while Sam and the girls settled for milk and some of Mom's homemade doughnuts.

The sun had barely risen over the woods across the pond the next morning when Sam was up. Sara could hear him coming out of his room across the hall. She leaned over in bed and shook Amy's shoulder that humped up under the bedclothes.

"Amy," she said in a loud whisper. "Sam's up. Do you want to go to the barn and help look for clues?"

Amy moaned sleepily. "Mnn? Oh ... sure." Yawning widely, she sat up in bed.

The girls slipped into their jeans and sweaters. Not wanting to awaken the other members of the family, they slipped quietly down the back stairs and out the side door. When they arrived at the barn, they found Sam standing in the middle of the threshing floor, gazing up at the lofts.

Amy's eyes widened as she looked around her. "You sure did clean this place out."

"We're using it as a garage now," Sara said, gesturing to the station wagon, Tim's VW jalopy, and the secondhand tractor and cultivator they had bought from Mr. Raber that summer. "Dad's using it for a workshop, too," she added, pointing to the workbench underneath one of the lofts.

"Why don't you girls search the stable while I climb up to the lofts," Sam suggested, handing Sara the pocket flash.

Sara led the way down the narrow wooden steps at the back of the threshing floor. Because their barn was a bank barn, it was dim in the stables, the lower part having been built into a hillside with the only windows facing the woods and pond. Sara was glad for Sam's flashlight.

The girls looked inside the stalls and examined the rusty old stanchions. They even peered inside the mangers and feed boxes. Amy paused by a stall that still had a matting of straw strewn over the floor.

"This was Bumper's stall when he lived here," she said in a low voice. She ran her hand lovingly over the stall door and looked back into the empty stall.

Sara walked on, flashing her light down at the stone floor and then at the back of the stable that had been built into the hillside. Although the outer walls of the barn were made of gray fieldstone, the wall built into the hillside was made of heavy wooden timbers. The round beam of the flashlight raked the wooden boards, but there was nothing there except a blank wall.

Finally the girls gave up their search and clambered up the steps to the threshing floor. Sam climbed down from the loft, his auburn hair tossed every which way and full of whisps of hay.

The girls couldn't help giggling, and Sara blurted out, "Sam, with that hay stuck all over you, you look like a scarecrow."

"Hey, thanks for the compliment, Madame Spider," Sam returned. "Better get that cobweb out of your own hair." In the next breath he asked, "Have you girls found anything?"

The girls shook their heads. "The stable's as clean as a whistle," Amy replied. "We couldn't even find a footprint."

"I didn't find anything, either," Sam admitted. "Whoever was prowling around here last night didn't leave any clues, that's for sure. What do we do now?"

"Forget about the old barn and hunt for the treasure," Sara said eagerly. "But first let's have breakfast. I'm starved, aren't you, Amy?"

Amy nodded and they walked back to the kitchen.

It was the custom for everybody in the Harmon family to make his own breakfast and lunch on Saturdays so that Mom could have the day off too. Sam brought out several cereal boxes and Sara poured the orange juice. They discovered some doughnuts still left in the pantry and sat down to eat. Before they finished, the telephone rang. Sara leaped up from the table and hurried into the hall to answer it. When she returned, she had a look of disappointment on her face.

"We'll have to delay hunting for the treasure," she explained. "That was Vickie calling. She wants Amy and me to come over to help her and Huy this morning. A gang of students just turned up from the college to go riding, and they're shorthanded."

"Where's Mike?" Sam asked.

"He had to help Mr. Raber take Beauty and Black Cloud to the Bucks County horse show this morning."

"Then we'll just have to help out," Amy said. "We can hunt for the treasure this afternoon."

"While you're at Fox Ridge Farm, I'll zip into town and see Kenny Pinto," Sam told them as they cleaned off their dishes and stacked them in the dishwasher. "His family just got a home computer that he wants to show me."

A short time later the girls got their bikes out of the barn and pedaled down the road. As they turned into Fox Ridge Farm, Sara said, "It looks as if we're really needed. Look at those cars parked by the corral."

A frantic Vickie met them at the corral gate. "Am I glad to see you two," she said. "Huy and I are saddling the horses. Could you help us?"

"Sure," the girls chorused.

There were twelve students, all eager to mount the six horses Huy and the girls led from the stable. Huy took the two more experienced riders up the ridge trail while Sara and Amy led four others around the trails which crossed the fields. The other six students slouched against the corral fence, talking with Vickie while they awaited their turn.

Toward noon the riders were all taken care of, and Dusty and Bumper had had enough exercise for one day. So the girls said good-bye to Vickie and Huy and started for home.

"It's good to ride Bumper and Dusty and feel useful at the same time," Amy said with satisfaction as they cycled down the lane.

Sara nodded. "I'm glad we could help out, but I'm also glad Mike will be back this afternoon so that we can start searching for that treasure."

Sam wandered home for lunch, and as they sat down to soup and sandwiches, Sara said, "Where do you think we should start looking for the treasure?"

"Here in the house, of course," Sam answered. "We could start with the attic and work down. It's more systematic that way."

Sara laughed at her twin. Leave it to Sam to be systematic, even in a treasure hunt.

As soon as they finished lunch, they trooped upstairs and walked down the hall to the narrow door at the end. Amy, who knew the third floor of the old house better than the

61

twins, lifted the old-fashioned door latch and led the way up the dim narrow steps to the low-roofed attic. She pulled a cord hanging down from the ceiling and a bare light bulb flashed on.

The twins glanced around them at the pile of packing boxes their father had placed in the middle of the floor the day they had moved into the old stone house. Other than the boxes and several pieces of old furniture that Amy said her parents had to leave behind because there was no room for them in the little house in town, the attic was bare.

Amy walked over to an antique walnut desk and fingered it lovingly. "Daddy knows a lot about antiques. He said this old desk was in the family as long ago as the 1760s. It's really called a secretary because it has a little bookcase on top."

"Oh," murmured Sara admiringly. It was a beautiful piece of furniture with four lower drawers and a hinged slant top which Amy opened to reveal an array of small drawers and pigeonholes. The slant top was a writing board equipped with a modern-day blotter.

"Daddy had said he would finish this old desk for me and I could have it in my room," Amy told them wistfully. "But then he lost his job and when Mama got sick I guess he forgot all about the secretary; so it was just left up here when we moved."

"Well, we'll take good care of it for you until your father can finish it," Sara promised. "It'll make a wonderful place to write and to keep your books." Secretly she wished there were two such desks in the attic and that she could have one for her room, too.

Sam turned away from the old secretary and looked around him. "We came here to hunt for the treasure, you know," he reminded the girls.

"I know, but first I want to look at this desk some more,"

Sara said. "Those little drawers are fascinating."

"I'll open them for you," Amy offered.

"Think of all the things you could keep in them," Sara said as Amy opened the first little drawer. It was empty as were the others, but the girls went on inspecting the old desk while Sam walked around, peering into the shadowy corners of the attic.

"I want to show you this," Amy said as she pulled out two decorative pillars on either side of a little door in the center of the desk.

"What are they used for?" asked Sara, noticing that they were hollow.

"They are letter holders," Amy replied. "Daddy said

"Think of all the things you could keep in these little drawers," Sara said.

people used to keep their correspondence in them."

Sara examined the hollow spaces in the pillars. "They're even long enough for business envelopes," she observed.

"And here's something else," Amy said, her eyes sparkling. "Open the little center door, Sara."

Sara did so, and behind the door were two more drawers topped by small pigeonholes. As she stooped to examine them, a thorough inspection showed that the drawers and small cubby holes had little depth compared to the letter holders alongside them.

"There must be a space behind these little drawers," she told Amy, "and there must be a way to get to it."

Amy frowned down at the long letter holders and then at the depth of the pigeonholes. "You're right. They're only half as deep as the letter holders. Daddy and I never noticed that."

The girls ran their fingers over the drawers and the pigeonholes and discovered that they were solidly framed. Looking closer at the unit, Amy said, "I believe this whole thing can be pulled out."

The girls took turns, carefully tugging at the center unit, but it remained firm. They tried to peer into the dark, narrow spaces on either side that the letter holders left, but the spaces were too long and narrow for them to see much.

"Maybe if we take out the drawers," Sara suggested, "we could see better." She drew out one drawer, but it wouldn't come out all the way.

Amy tried the other one, and when she drew it out as far as it would go, the girls heard a soft click. They stared at each other with surprise when the center unit slid out easily.

Behind it, in a secret niche, were three more small drawers of unfinished blond wood, just big enough to hold keys or coins or jewels.

Sara let out a squeal of surprise. "A secret compartment!"

Amy's eyes were bright with curiosity. "I had heard that old desks often had secret drawers and things," she exclaimed, "but I never thought this one had."

Sam, who had been knocking on the attic walls to hunt for hollow spaces, stopped his search and hurried over to the old walnut secretary. "Hey, what's all the excitement about?" he asked.

"Look, Sam, we found a secret compartment," Sara explained, pointing to the three blond drawers.

Sam jerked erect and drew in a deep breath. "Hey, maybe this is where Adam Goodwin hid his treasure!"

"That's what I'm thinking," Amy said, her voice tense with excitement.

"You open them, Amy," Sara said. "After all, it's your desk and your treasure."

"I'm almost afraid to," the girl replied in a taut whisper. She reached out a trembling hand and slowly drew open the top drawer. Sara and Sam peered over her shoulder, then looked at each other with disappointment. The drawer was empty.

"Try the other two," urged Sam.

Amy slowly drew out the middle drawer but it, too, was empty.

"Well, it must be in the bottom drawer," Sara said, trying her best to make her voice sound optimistic. "Pull it out."

Amy cringed back as if afraid to try a third time.

"I can't. You do it," she pleaded in a choked voice.

Sam didn't waste time. He reached over her shoulder and pulled out the last drawer. When they peered into it, it appeared to be empty also. Sam groaned and was about to slide it back into the niche when Sara grabbed his wrist. "Wait a sec, Sam, I think the bottom's lined with something."

Sam handed her the drawer, and Sara took it over to the light to examine it. Sure enough, lining the bottom of the drawer was a tightly folded piece of paper. With trembling hands she wedged it out with her fingernails. It was yellowed with age and looked very old.

Sam and Amy hurried to her side. "What is it?" they asked in unison. Then when they saw the folded square of paper they cried, "Open it up, Sara!"

7

The Code Message

Sara's hands worked nervously as she opened the tightly folded paper. She laid it on the writing board of the old secretary and smoothed it out so that they could see it better. They took a look at the thin, spidery writing then stared at one another incredulously.

"I can't read it!" were Amy's bewildered words.

"Neither can I," replied Sara.

Sam's lip curled in an exaggerated pout as he squinted down at the many rows of faded letters that didn't make any sense.

Finally Sam said, "It's just lines of mixed up letters run together, but I think I know what it is."

"What?" the girls chorused.

```
V J K U K U Y T K V V G P K P E Q F G U Q V J
C V Q P N A A Q W T G A G U E C P T G C F K V
G N K B C D G V J K J C X G D G G P V C M G P
R T K U Q P G T D G E C W U G K J G N R G F E
Q N Q P G N Y K N M G U C D T K V K U J Q H H
K E G T T G E Q X G T H T Q O Y Q W P F U D A
J K F K P I J K O K P Q W T D C T P K P T G V
W T P H Q T O A H C X Q T U J G R T G U G P V
G F O G Y K V J C F K C O Q P F T K P I C H C
O K N A J G K T N Q Q O D G E C W U G K U C X
G F J K U N K H G J G K P U K U V G F K V C M
G K V C N V J Q W I J K V Q N F J K O Y G H T
K G P F U F Q P Q V D G N K G X G K P Q T P C
O G P V K P I Q W T U G N X G U Y K V J H K P
G T A K J C X G J K F F G P V J G T K P I K P
V J G E J K O P G A K V U J Q W N F D G Y Q T
V J C U O C N N H Q T V W P G U G N N K V K H
A Q W P G G F O Q P G A I Q F D N G U U A Q W
F G C T G N K B C D G V J C P F Q W T U Q P A
Q W T H C K V J H W N C P F N Q X K P I J W U
D C P F C F O
```

"It's a message written in secret code. We'll have to break the code before we can read it."

"A secret code!" Sara exclaimed, her eyes agleam with interest. "How are we going to break it?"

"By using our noodles," Sam grinned, tapping his head with his knuckles. "Let's take it down to my room and see if we can figure it out."

"Why would a note written in code be hidden in the secret compartment of the secretary?" Amy asked breathlessly as they hurried down the attic steps.

"I don't know," Sam flung back over his shoulder. "Maybe someone didn't want the message to be known."

"It looks awfully old," Amy said. "It must have been written a long time ago."

"It sure is mysterious," Sara added, jittery with excitement. A secret message, written in code, and hidden in the antique secretary! Sara thought it was almost as exciting as finding the treasure.

When they arrived at Sam's room, he switched on his desk lamp, and they hovered over the mysterious message. "I wish I could put this in a computer," Sam said. "If the letters weren't all run together, but formed into words, it would be easier to figure out."

They puzzled over the code message until the letters swam around in Sara's head. At last she straightened up with a long sigh and said, "I can't think any longer. Let's look around some more for that treasure, Amy."

The girls spent the rest of the afternoon searching the attic, but they couldn't find anything that even resembled a hidden treasure. By dinnertime Sam gave up on the code, too. But all through dinner he sat quietly with that faraway look in his eyes, the look he always wore when he had a problem to solve.

His family didn't question him because they all knew from experience that it wouldn't do any good to ask Sam what he was thinking about. He would be so engrossed in his problem that he wouldn't hear them anyway. So they turned their attention to their guest.

"We'll be going to church tomorrow," Mrs. Harmon said. "Would you like to come with us, Amy?"

Amy looked uncertain, as if she didn't know how to answer. "I'm not a member of the church and neither are my parents," she said in a small voice.

"One doesn't have to be a member to go to church," Mrs. Harmon told her. "A church is open to everyone."

"I know you'll like our church," Sara urged. "And Pastor Reese is real neat."

"He's president of the Maplewood Historical Society," her father added, "and knows more about the early history of Maplewood than anybody in town. After the service we could ask him about your ancestor, Amy. He may know something about Adam Goodwin that would be helpful in writing your American history essay."

Amy looked up from the table. "All right," she said with an answering smile. "I'll go."

As they walked down the church aisle the next morning, Sara could feel Alison Heston's eyes fixed on her and Amy. Well, let her stare, Sara thought defiantly as they sat down in their pew. Who cares what old Alison thinks. Amy's my friend and I don't care who knows it!

At the end of the service when they were shaking Pastor Reese's hand, Sara introduced Amy. "So you are a Goodwin?" the minister asked in his friendly voice. "The Goodwins are one of our oldest families in Maplewood. I believe Adam Goodwin was one of the first to settle here."

Amy looked up at the minister, pride showing in her eyes. "Then you do know about him?" she asked.

"I know that Adam Goodwin was a Friend and helped to build the first Friends Meetinghouse in Maplewood," Pastor Reese answered.

"We're writing an essay about Adam Goodwin for the American history project at school," Sara explained quickly, "and we'd like to find out all we can about him."

The gentle gray-haired minister smiled. "I suppose you did some research at the library?"

The girls nodded. The minister then added, "Have you examined the records of the Friends Meeting?"

The girls looked at each other and shook their heads.

"Well, I think that would be an excellent place to look," Pastor Reese suggested. "I'm a friend of Mr. Harrison, the Clerk of the Meeting. I'd be glad to introduce you to him. Suppose I call him and set a date."

They were surprised when the phone rang right after dinner, and it was Pastor Reese, calling to tell them that Mr. Harrison would see them that very afternoon. Professor Harmon, who was interested in knowing more about the Friends Meeting, offered to drive the girls into Maplewood, and Sam went along. They stopped by the parsonage to pick up Pastor Reese, who directed them to the old stone meetinghouse on the far side of town.

The Clerk of the Meeting was a small, thin man with white hair and watery eyes who said he had served the Meeting for forty years. He led them into his office, and producing a key from his pocket, he opened a glass bookcase where the records were kept. He pulled out a large black book and opened it. Running his wrinkled fingers down the list of names on the first page, he stopped at the name Goodwin and handed the book to Amy.

"I think you'll find everything you want to know about Adam Goodwin in this book," he said. Then he left the young people to their research and ushered Professor Harmon and Pastor Reese into the main part of the meetinghouse.

The girls opened their notebooks and began jotting down items of interest, including a list of Adam Goodwin's ancestors in England. There was even a tie-in with the Penn family, which Sam thought interesting, but Amy and Sara were more interested in Adam himself.

"Listin to this." Sara read, " 'The first meeting of the Friends was held in Adam Goodwin's farmhouse in 1769. Later, when more Friends settled in Maplewood, the stone meetinghouse was built in 1774.' "

"That's something for our essay," Amy said, writing down the information.

Peering intently at the book, Sara's eyes sparkled with lively interest. "And here's the name of Henry Tyler, the Friend who Adam confided in when he hid Colonel Wilkes. It says that when Elizabeth returned from Philadelphia, Henry Tyler told her all about Adam caring for the English colonel. He also helped Elizabeth try to get Adam released from prison."

They jotted down Henry Tyler's name, then read on.

"Oh, look at this!" Amy's voice rose to an excited pitch. She read, " 'Adam Goodwin's farm had a hiding place for Friends who were being persecuted for being pacifists.' "

"That's neat!" Sara exclaimed as she scribbled down the information in her notebook. "I wonder if that was where Adam hid the colonel while he was recovering from his wounds."

Amy pursed her lips thoughtfully. "My family and I had never heard of a hiding place on the farm," she said with a puzzled shake of her head. "I wonder where it was."

They read silently for a while, but all the other information was exactly like the account of Adam Goodwin that they had found at the public library and in the Goodwin family Bible.

Amy finally looked up from the book. "Not one mention of Adam's treasure," she said dejectedly.

Sara thought a moment, her lip caught between her teeth. "Maybe Adam hid his treasure in the hiding place mentioned in this book," she suggested.

"Wherever that hiding place is," Amy answered with a sigh.

All this while Sam had been quiet. Now he spoke up in a thoughtful voice. "I can't get that secret code out of my mind. I keep thinking that if we could decipher it, we might get some answers. Maybe it would tell us something about the treasure and the hiding place."

Amy cheered up a little at that. "Oh, do you think so!" she exclaimed. Then her voice fell as she remembered, "But we can't break the code."

8

Footsteps in the Barn

The next morning before they left for school, Sara went to Sam's room for the code message. Excitement coursed through her at the idea she had of how they might be able to decode it. She had planned to go to the library after school to see if there was any information about secret codes. It would be neat if she could find a book that would explain how to break the code message they had found in secretary.

She folded the wrinkled, yellowed paper and carefully placed it in her math book. It may come in handy in her search for the right code book, she decided. She may even be able to figure out the code while at the library. Wouldn't Sam be surprised!

Later that morning, in social studies, Mrs. Bailey announced that they had until next Monday to complete their essays for the American history project.

A groan rippled through the class, and Alison Heston spoke up in a pleading voice, "Couldn't we have longer than that? Please, Mrs. Bailey?"

The teacher remained firm. "We have much to cover this semester, and that's all the time I can give you for this project. Besides," she smiled knowingly at the class, "if I gave you as long as a month, I doubt if you'd start working on your essays before the last week."

"Aw, Mrs. Bailey," several voices groaned. "Have a heart!"

"I have one," bantered the teacher, "and it's in fine condition, thank you. Now, I suggest you all get started on your essays before it's too late."

Her final words sent a solemn hush through the class, and Sara had the feeling that everyone knew the teacher meant business. Faces were serious when the buzzer sounded and the class filed out of the room.

"Do you think we can have our essay done in a week?" Amy asked with concern as they made their way to the cafeteria. "It's going to be tough working on the secret code and hunting for the treasure at the same time."

"We'll divide the work," Sara suggested. "Why don't you start organizing our notes while Sam and I try to break the code."

Amy nodded agreement. "That's the advantage of working as a team, but I don't know which one of us will have the harder job."

"They'll both be hard, and that's why we have to get down to work right now. Thank goodness the other teachers are going easy on the homework."

"They'll make up for it after this week," Amy predicted.

75

"Then it'll be Mrs. Bailey's turn to ease up—I hope!"

After school Sara made her way to the library. A flock of ninth-graders had already gathered at the reserve shelf, searching for material. Sara didn't find the card catalog any less crowded. She opened the "C" drawer and riffled through the cards, looking for the word "Code."

"Looks as if old Bailey's words got through to everybody," a familiar voice spoke over her shoulder.

Sara swung around and came face to face with Doug Cooper, the blond boy who had sat across from her that day in the cafeteria when she had felt so down. Even though his handsome grin made her heart do a flip-flop, she was not as out of control with him this time as she had been when they first met.

"She really shook up the class," Sara agreed with a bob of her head. "Is she usually like that?"

"Always," Doug answered with a grin, "but even so, she's one of the most popular teachers at Maplewood. It's her enthusiasm for the subject that comes across. Even if you're not that keen on social studies, she makes it kind of exciting. Like this American history project. She's got us all psyched up on it today, and we won't come down to earth again until the essays are handed in."

"You're a pretty good judge of character," Sara heard herself saying in a flattering tone.

Doug blushed modestly. "Oh, I've just been around here longer than you." Changing the subject away from himself, he said, "So you and Amy are writing about Adam Goodwin?"

It was Sara's turn to feel flustered. "That's right," she admitted. Then in a firmer tone she added, "My family and I live at the old Goodwin place now, and Amy is our friend."

"I know," Doug replied. "You ought to make a good

team." He paused then said, "Well, I got to get back to work." And using his favorite expression, he added, "See ya around."

Sara smiled as she watched his blond head disappear through the gathering of students. She was glad that she had found another friend at Maplewood High and that it was Doug Cooper.

Turning back to the card catalog, she glimpsed Sam and another boy poring over the cards in the file drawers directly across from her. She called over in a loud whisper, "Have you found a topic yet, Sam?"

Her twin looked up, all smiles. "Sure have. Kenny and I are writing about the iron industry in colonial Maplewood. Did you know that Alison Heston's ancestor, Major Benjamin Heston, was the first ironmaster? Oh, by the way, Twinny, this is Kenny Pinto. Kenny, my sister, Sara."

Kenny nodded a brief greeting. He had dark curly hair and brown, inquiring eyes that peered at her vaguely from behind a pair of horn-rimmed glasses. Just Sam's type, Sara thought, smiling to herself as she nodded back at Kenny. The boys bent their heads together again over the catalog drawer, and Sara returned to her own work.

She was disappointed to find only one book on codes, called *Codes and Deciphering*, listed in the card catalog. Fortunately the book was on the shelf, so she took it to one of the reading tables and curiously leafed through the pages. She soon discovered that there were so many codes mentioned that it made her head spin.

There was a chapter explaining how numbers were substituted for letters. There were position codes where the position of a line or a dot stood for a letter. There were code wheels and even multiplication codes.

Sara spread out the code message they had found in the

old secretary, but none of these codes seemed to apply to it. She was beginning to wonder if their code message had been written in a secret code which would be impossible to decipher.

Discouraged, she was about to close the book and let Sam figure it all out when something on the next page caught her eye. She leaned over the table and peered intently at the page before her. It described the principle of substituting one letter of the alphabet for another by letting *a* be *b* and *b* be *c* and so on. The example of the code the book gave looked exactly like their code.

Sara was so absorbed in what she was reading that she didn't notice Amy making her way to her table. Not until Amy pointed to the library book and asked, "What's that?" did Sara look up with a start.

"It's a book on codes," Sara said. "And guess what, I think I have discovered the secret code used in the message we found in the secretary. Now all we have to do is to read how to decode it."

"Great!" Amy replied. "I turned up a few more things that we missed the first time we looked through those reference books. I think now we have all the information we need to write our essay."

Sara put the code message in *Codes and Deciphering*, and checked the library book out at the circulation desk.

"You know, I believe every kid in our class was here today," Amy observed as they were leaving the library.

"All except Alison," Sara reminded her. "She has cheerleading practice every day after school."

"Could be she's getting all her information from Major Heston's diary," Amy said.

"Could be," echoed Sara. "With a diary crammed full of information, she won't have to study reference books."

When they reached Amy's garage where Sara had parked her bicycle that morning, they noticed that it was occupied by a blue Ford.

"Daddy's home," Amy announced. "I guess he didn't go to the hospital today."

As Sara put her library book into the carrying basket attached to the handlebars, she wished that Amy was coming home with her again. It would be so much easier to write their essay if they were together. She looked up at her friend with questioning eyes and put her thoughts into words.

Amy must have been thinking the same thing because with a quick smile she said. "I'll ask Daddy. Come on in."

Mr. Goodwin, dressed in a blue shirt and work pants, got up from the dining room table when he heard them come into the house. Sara saw that his hair was graying and his face was drawn and haggard. Even though he smiled politely when Amy introduced Sara, his smile couldn't hide the little worry lines around his mouth. Still, his deep gray eyes brightened when he looked fondly at his daughter.

"I guess it will be all right to spend the week with the Harmons, if they don't mind," he said. Sara assured him that her parents wouldn't mind at all.

While Amy ran upstairs to pack a bag, Mr. Goodwin looked apologetically at Sara. "I'd say you could spend the week here with Amy, then you'd be closer to school. But with Amy's mother in the hospital, things are somewhat disorganized around here."

"How is Mrs. Goodwin?" Sara asked.

"Oh, she's getting a little better each day, but the doctor says it'll be a while yet before she can come home. And when she does, she'll have to take it easy. Amy and I will have to take good care of her."

"I'm sure you will," Sara said, smiling.

Amy bounced down the stairs with her overnight bag. "You're sure you'll be all right here alone, Daddy?" she asked with concern.

Mr. Goodwin nodded. "I'm sure, honey. I'll be spending most of my time at the hospital anyway, and your mother will be glad to hear that you have a friend to be with this week."

As they cycled up the road to Marsh Pond Farm, Sara's heart went out to Amy's father. She couldn't help thinking how much easier his life would be if he believed that God was there to help him.

When they arrived at the farm and wheeled their bikes into the barn, Sara noticed Sam's red ten-speed at its usual place under the loft by their father's workbench.

"Sam beat us home," she remarked as they parked their bikes alongside his.

They were taking their books out of their baskets when they heard something that made them turn to stare at each other with puzzled eyes. Then they heard it again—the sound of a footstep on the stairs leading down into the stable.

Sara put her library book on her father's workbench and forced herself to walk back to the dark stairway. "Sam?" she called.

She was answered by the sound of more furtive footsteps skittering across the stone floor below them. Puzzled, she called again, "Sam, is that you?"

The footsteps stopped suddenly and a foreboding hush settled over the dim stable.

Amy slipped over to Sara's side and grasped her arm. "Do you think it's the prowlers again?" she whispered in a trembling voice.

"I don't know," Sara's own shaky voice whispered back.

80

"Let's find my mom."

The girls fled from the barn to the house.

"Mom," Sara called when they rushed into the big cosy kitchen. But there was no answer.

"Mom! Sam! Anybody home?" she called, much louder this time. But her voice disappeared through the empty house.

Sara took an uneven breath and said, "Mom's probably out in the shed, painting, and Sam's probably with her. Come on, Amy, let's find them."

The girls hurried from the house and across the field to the shed. They found Mrs. Harmon holding a stepladder

Sara forced herself to walk back to the dark stairway. "Sam?" she called. "Sam, is that you?"

while Sam was perched on top, hanging one of his mother's paintings on the studio wall.

"A little to the left, Sam," Mrs. Harmon directed. When she turned and saw the girls, she exclaimed, "Why, Sara—Amy, what's the matter? You're all out of breath."

"Someone's in the barn again," Sara burst out.

"We heard footsteps in the stable," Amy panted.

Mrs. Harmon looked shocked for a moment. Then she said in a reasonably calm voice, "Well, let's have a look. Sam and I are about ready to leave anyway."

Sam got down from the ladder and Mrs. Harmon cleaned her brushes. Before leaving the shed, she locked the door carefully.

"I don't like the idea of prowlers in our barn," she said as they made their way across the field. "What could anyone be doing in there?"

"That's what we'd like to know," Sara replied.

They were approaching the barn as Tim's VW came rumbling up the drive. With a shout Sam hailed it and Tim brought his jalopy to a halt.

"Sara and Amy heard someone prowling around in the barn this afternoon," Mrs. Harmon told her older son. "Did you see anybody around here when you drove up?"

Tim frowned and shook his head. "Only people I saw this afternoon were Vickie and Huy." He paused, then grinned. "Oh, yeah. I passed Pete Simmons in that red Chevette of his as I drove out of the Raber's lane. He had his girl with him. She sure is cute."

Sara and Amy exchanged knowing glances.

"That girl is Alison Heston," Amy explained. "She latched on to Pete when he went out for football this year."

"But they're supposed to be at football and cheerleading practice," Sara said with a puzzled shake of her head.

Tim grinned. "Boy, they must have it bad to skip practice so that they can be together."

Sam was listening to all this with an impatient look on his face. At last he broke in, "Let's get back to the subject at hand and look inside the barn."

They followed him down the steps to the stable where the girls had heard the footsteps. They searched behind the stanchions and around the mangers and feed boxes but, like before, they found no signs of the prowlers. When they returned to the threshing floor, Mrs. Harmon gave the girls a searching look and asked, "Are you *sure* you heard some-one down there?"

Sara nodded, then added, "Of course, whoever was here had plenty of time to leave while we went to the shack to get you and Sam."

"Maybe some animal got into the barn and that's what you heard," Tim suggested. "A chipmunk got in here one day last summer while I was working on the VW, and, man, it sounded just like a human rustling around."

Mrs. Harmon turned to the girls, her eyes questioning. "Do you think it could have been some kind of animal?" she asked hopefully.

Sara and Amy looked at each other. "Well—maybe," they relented.

But as they were leaving the barn and Sara went to the workbench to pick up her library book, she stopped short and let out a surprised cry.

"Now I know someone's been here," she gasped. "And it wasn't any animal, either."

She pointed a trembling finger to the library book that lay open on the workbench. The secret code that she had tucked inside the book was gone.

9

Adam Goodwin's Message

It's a good thing I made an extra copy of the code," Sam said on the way back to the house.

"Oh, Sam! You did?" Amy exclaimed, her mouth dropping open with happy surprise.

Sam gave her a big lopsided smile and nodded. "Sure. I wanted a copy for myself, so that I wouldn't have to pester you girls every time I wanted to work on it."

"Oh, Sam, you're a lifesaver," Sara squealed. "Where is it?"

"Up in my room. Come on, I'll show you. And bring that book you got from the library, Sara. Mom said Dad has a faculty meeting and will be home late, so we'll have some time before dinner to work on the code."

While the girls got comfortable on Sam's bed, Sam opened his desk drawer and drew out the copy of the code message he had made. As he handed it to them, he said, "It beats me who would want to take the code message from your library book, Sara."

"It must be those prowlers," Sara speculated. "Only I don't know why they are so fascinated with our barn or why they would want the code message."

Sam drew his brows together as he considered the matter. "Maybe they're hunting for something in the barn and when they saw the code message in the library book, they may have thought it would help them to find what they're looking for."

"But what can they be looking for?" piped Amy. She pondered her question a moment then drew in her breath. "Do you think they know about the treasure and are searching for that?"

Sam shrugged. "Could be. Let's see if we can beat them in breaking the code. What did you find in the library book, Sara, that you thought was so important?"

Sara turned to the chapter on code wheels and explained the principle of substituting one letter of the alphabet for another. She pointed to an illustration of two alphabet strips.

"Both strips have the alphabet printed on them," she explained. "But the longer strip has the alphabet printed twice. By sliding the shorter strip along the edge of the longer one, *a* could mean any other letter in the alphabet. If *a* was set over *g*, then *b* would become *h* and *c* would become *i* and so on."

"I get it!" Amy cried. The next moment she brought her brows together in a quick frown. "But where do we start? *A* could be any letter."

Sara bit the knuckle of her forefinger and brooded over

the code message. "If these lines of letters were divided into words, we could experiment with one group at a time, like three letters could mean *and* or *the* and one letter could be *a* or *I*."

"Yeah, but with the letters running together, we have to work with one at a time," Sam said, pushing his shaggy auburn hair out of his eyes, "and that's going to be difficult. Give me your book, Sara."

Sara handed him *Codes and Deciphering*, and Sam gave the page she had turned to a concentrated look. Suddenly his face lighted up. "Hey, listen to this! It says that the most frequently used letter in the alphabet is *e* and the next is *t*. It gives a list of letters in order of use."

He swung around on his chair and began searching through the pile of papers and books on his desk. At last he found a tablet and a pencil and began to copy the list. He wrote:

E T A O N R I S H D L F C M U G Y P W B V K X J Q Z

"How can that help us?" Amy wondered.

"We'll count the number of times each letter is used in the message," Sam replied eagerly. "I'll read them off, and you girls copy them down. Each time the letter I read is used, put a mark behind it."

Hastily the two girls grabbed pencil and paper, and Sam started to read slowly each letter of the secret code, starting with the first letter in the code which was *v*. When he was through reading the letters, they counted the number of times each letter was used and discovered that *g* was used the most times. *V* came next, then *c*, *q*, and *p*.

"Let's assume that *g* is *e*, *v* is *t*, *c* is *a*, *q* is *o*, and *p* is *n*," Sam suggested. "We'll make two alphabet strips, like the ones in the book, one longer than the other and see what we get."

Rummaging through the pencils and papers in his desk drawer, he found a pair of scissors and cut two strips of paper, one longer than the other. While he studied the code before him, the girls copied the letters in the alphabet on the strips.

"Now," Sam said, "slide the letter *g* on the longer strip under the letter *e* on the shorter strip. Like this:

A	B	C	D	E	F	G	H	I	J	K	L	M	N	O	P	Q	R	S	T	U	V	W	X	Y	Z
C	D	E	F	G	H	I	J	K	L	M	N	O	P	Q	R	S	T	U	V	W	X	Y	Z	A	B

"That makes the first letter in the message a *t*," Amy pointed out."

By transposing the letters, the first line of the code became:

T H I S I S W R I T T E N I N C O D E S O T H

"Now all we have to do is to divide the letters into words," Sam said, his voice cracking with excitement. "We'll break this secret code yet!"

He bent his head over the first line in the code message and drew lines between the letters which formed words. When he finished, the line read:

THIS IS WRITTEN IN CODE SO TH

"It works!" cried Amy, beaming at Sam. Forgetting her shyness, she went on, "Oh, Sam, you're a genius! Maybe you ought to be a cryptographer for the government instead of a computer scientist."

Sam blushed furiously and mumbled, "We couldn't have done it without Sara's library book. Come on, let's figure out the rest of the message."

Just then Mom's cowbell sounded from the kitchen below, summoning them for dinner.

"Oh, bother! We would have to go down now, just when we're about to discover what the message reads," Sara grumbled.

Sam put the book and code message on his desk and switched off his desk lamp. Before they left the room he said, "Right after dinner we'll meet here. Okay?"

They nodded solemn agreement and followed him out the door.

Professor and Mrs. Harmon were delighted to have Amy spend the week with them, and all through dinner they listened with rapt attention while the girls and Sam explained about finding the code message in the old secretary in the attic and how they had just discovered a way to decipher it.

"Sounds interesting," Professor Harmon said, pushing his empty dinner plate aside. He looked over at the young people and gave them a wink. "Let's hurry through dessert, Janice," he told his wife, "so that our cryptographers can find out what that message says."

Sara gave her father a grateful smile as she leaped up from the table to help Mom serve the apple pie.

A short time later the three were in Sam's room again, bending their heads over the secret code.

"Let's divide the lines," Amy suggested. "That way we can get the message decoded faster."

The twins nodded agreement and with paper and pencil they set to work. Because the code message was so long, it took them a good half hour to decode their lines and to di-

88

vide them into words. Sam finished first and helped the girls. At last all the lines were decoded, and they put them together so that they could read the entire message. Sam pored over the secret code and read it aloud.

This is written in code so that only your eyes can read it, Elizabeth. I have been taken prisoner because I helped Colonel Wilkes, a British officer, recover from wounds by hiding him in our barn. In return for my favors, he presented me with a diamond ring, a family heirloom. Because I saved his life, he insisted I take it although I told him we Friends do not believe in ornamenting ourselves with finery. I have hidden the ring in the chimney. It should be worth a small fortune. Sell it if you need money. God bless you, dear Elizabeth, and our son. Your faithful and loving husband, Adam.

For a moment the three young people were silent. Then Amy turned to Sara and Sam with sparkling eyes. "I always had the feeling that there was a treasure hidden here somewhere, and now we know there really is one."

"And where it is hidden," added Sara, her eyes round with excitement.

"So Adam had left Elizabeth a note, telling her all about the treasure," Sam mused. "And he wrote it in code so that only she could read it."

Sara went on, "The note says that he hid the ring in the chimney. Does that mean we'll have to search the two big chimneys on either end of the house?"

Sam shook his head. "I believe in the old days people referred to fireplaces as chimneys. Most likely he hid the ring behind a brick in one of our fireplaces. Let's ask Dad."

The three showed the code message to Professor Harmon, who dropped his evening paper with interest.

Mrs. Harmon put her book aside and joined them. "I

can't see how anything could be hidden in a chimney," she said skeptically.

Her husband had an answer for that. "In the old days the chimney around the hearth was a favorite hiding place, Janice. Money, jewelry, and even deeds to land were often put behind bricks to keep them safe from fire and theft. Chimneys were our first safes."

Sara looked up at the enormous brick fireplace that took up most of the wall space at the end of the living room. "Does that mean we have to search every brick?"

Her father nodded. "I suppose so." He arose from his chair and led the way to the fireplace.

"Look for loose mortar," he explained. "Then see if the brick can be lifted out." His eyes twinkled. "I'll help you search for the ring. I haven't been on a treasure hunt since I was a boy."

Mrs. Harmon joined in the search, too, and they set to work, running their fingers over the mortar of each brick. It took a long time, even with the five of them searching.

"I never knew there were so many bricks in a fireplace," Sam groaned impatiently.

"Well, this is just what Mrs. Bailey wants us to do," Sara told him. "Snoop around unlikely places to dig out clues that will help us with our essays."

When they finished examining all the bricks and found nothing, Professor Harmon stood back and surveyed the fireplace with a thoughtful shake of his head. "You know, maybe Adam's wife took the ring from its hiding place and sold it for money to live on, as her husband wanted her to do."

Mrs. Harmon nodded slowly. "Most likely that's what happened."

"But there was always talk in Amy's family that Adam

Goodwin had hidden a treasure," Sara protested. "Why should all those generations of Goodwins have hunted for it if they didn't believe the treasure was still here?"

"You know what I think," Sam said seriously. "I think Elizabeth Goodwin didn't have the time or opportunity to sell the ring and left it where Adam had hidden it. Remember, she became ill and died of pneumonia shortly after her husband died in prison."

Amy brightened. "As Sara said, Elizabeth could have mentioned something about the treasure to Adam's parents, but not where it was hidden. That could be why my family knew about the treasure but were never able to find it."

Sara added, "And after Elizabeth read Adam's code message, she probably put it into the secret compartment of the old secretary for safekeeping, and nobody has found it until now."

"If that's so, then the diamond ring is still here somewhere," Sam concluded. His eyes sparkled as a thought struck him. "We haven't searched all the chimneys yet. There's another one in the kitchen."

"Not tonight," his mother spoke up, shaking her head. "It's getting late. Tomorrow after school will be a better time to search the chimney in the kitchen."

"Promise you won't look for the treasure until we get home?" Sara asked. "We want to be here when it's found."

Her mother nodded. "I promise. Now scoot."

All the while they were getting ready for bed, Amy looked worried. Sara studied her friend with concern. "What's the matter, Amy? If Adam's treasure is here, we'll find it."

"I know," Amy said, biting her lip. "What's bothering me is that someone else may be looking for it, too."

The two girls stared at each other.

"That's right!" Sara cried in dismay. "The person who

took the secret code from my library book. If the prowlers can figure out the code, then they'll know where the treasure is hidden. And whoever is prowling around in the barn can prowl around the house, too, when we're at school and Mom's at the shack, painting."

Amy's glance flew to the copy of the code message on Sara's desk. "I just wonder who it is, prowling around inside the barn," she said in a tight voice.

"Well, one thing I do know," Sara vowed. "Tomorrow after school, you and I are getting home as fast as we can to search that chimney in the kitchen."

10
Prowlers Again

Sara and Amy decided to take the bus to school the next morning. It would be quicker coming home by the school bus than riding their bicycles.

As the bus rumbled down the road toward Maplewood, the girls sat together in the backseat, preoccupied with their own thoughts. Sara kept thinking about the secret code they had deciphered and wondered if the chimney in the kitchen would reveal the hiding place of Adam's treasure. She hoped it would. She couldn't think of anything more fascinating to illustrate their essay with than a two hundred-year-old treasure that they had found, and Amy's family certainly could use the money the diamond ring would bring.

Sara was still thinking about the hidden treasure when

they arrived at school and she bumped into Doug Cooper in the hall by the lockers.

"Hi," Doug said, a smile twitching the corners of his lips. "Going to homeroom?"

Sara nodded. While she busied herself with her locker combination, Doug drew out a white envelope that had been stuck into the vent slot on top of the locker door.

"Looks like somebody left you a note," he said, handing her the envelope.

Sara stuck it inside her math book. "Probably a notice from the office," she said.

Slamming shut the locker door, she walked down the hall with Doug.

"How's the essay coming?" she asked, in way of conversation.

"I haven't even started writing it yet," Doug answered.

"What are you writing about?"

"Promise you won't laugh when I tell you?"

"Promise," Sara said.

"The old gristmill on Main Street."

"I don't believe it!" Sara exclaimed, giggling in spite of her promise not to laugh. "How did you pull that off? So many other kids wanted to write about it."

"I know," Doug replied, grinning, "but when Mrs. Bailey found out that my ancestor, Jonathan Wenzel, built that mill and was the first miller in Maplewood, she thought I should be the one to write about it. So at this point I'm going through a lot of old junk in a trunk in our attic, trying to find something belonging to Jonathan Wenzel that I could use as memorabilia. So far all I found was one of his old handknit socks."

Sara laughed. She was beginning to feel at ease with this tall, good-natured, blond boy, and she liked his sense of humor. Before she knew it, she was telling him about her and Amy's essay.

"I know how hard it is to find something hidden away for generations," she said. "We were lucky to find a message that Adam Goodwin wrote to his wife when he was taken a prisoner by Major Heston."

Sara winced at the thought that they no longer had the original code message. And if they couldn't find the diamond ring, there would be no memorabilia to help illustrate their essay.

Doug interrupted her thoughts by stopping right in the middle of the hall and looking down at her with surprise in his eyes.

"Adam Goodwin was taken a prisoner by Major Heston?" he asked. "What for? Was he a Tory?"

Sara shook her head. "No, he was a Quaker pacifist who saved the life of a wounded British officer."

"You mean Adam Goodwin went to prison for that?" Doug exclaimed.

"Not only did he go to prison, but he died there," Sara responded, smiling faintly. "Not much of a hero according to Maplewood standards, I guess."

"I don't know about that," Doug reflected. "In my mind any man who would risk his life to save the life of another man is the best kind of hero."

Sara smiled up at the tall boy by her side. "Oh, Doug, I'm glad to hear you say that because Amy and I think so too!"

At that moment the hall buzzer sounded, sending them scurrying to their homeroom. When they entered the classroom, Alison looked up as Sara passed her desk, then quickly looked away again. Sara ignored the unfriendly girl and sat down at her own desk behind Amy.

She opened her math book to finish the last two problems

for homework, and it was then that she spied the white envelope and remembered that Doug had pulled it out from the vent slot at the top of her locker. Expecting a notice from the office, she slit the envelope open with her pencil and was surprised as she pulled out a yellowed sheet of paper.

Her eyes fixed on the wrinkled old paper, she let out a gasp audible enough for Amy to turn around and stare at her. Sara pointed to the paper in her hand.

"It's the secret code!" she hissed.

Amy stared wide-eyed at Adam Goodwin's code message. "Where did you find it?"

"Someone left it in my locker door," Sara explained.

Amy gave her friend a puzzled look, as if she found it hard to believe that the missing code would be found in such an unlikely place as Sara's locker.

At that moment Mrs. Bailey entered the room and they had to stop talking. Sara carefully put the code message back into the envelope, but she kept thinking about it all through homeroom.

Whoever took the code and returned it must be someone here at school, she reasoned. Someone who knew where her locker was.

But why would anyone at Maplewood High want to prowl around their barn and take the code message from her library book? She and Amy were the only ones writing about Adam Goodwin. It just didn't make sense.

A lot of things don't make sense, Sara told herself as she tucked the envelope into her math book and got ready for her first class. The mystery of the secret code was getting more puzzling than ever.

"If it was someone from school who took the code, it must be someone who's involved with the American history project," Sam reasoned when Sara had told him about finding Adam's code message in her locker that morning.

It was after school and they were in the kitchen, exploring the bricks in the cavernous old fireplace with the brick oven alongside it. Sitting back on his heels, Sam went on, "It's strange, though, that whoever stole the code message would return it so quickly."

"Maybe they couldn't figure out the secret code and thought it was useless and a waste of time," Amy suggested.

"Well, whatever their reason, I'm glad they returned it," Sara said gratefully. "We need it to illustrate our essay, especially if we don't find the ring."

They continued their search of the kitchen chimney, carefully examining each brick. Once Amy called out that she had discovered a loose one, but when they managed to wiggle it free from the chimney, they found nothing behind it but loose mortar.

When they had examined the last row of bricks in the fireplace and had found nothing, Sara said, trying to keep discouragement from creeping into her voice, "Well, we tried our best. With our essays due next Monday, we better stop hunting for the treasure and finish organizing our notes so that we can start writing."

Sam kept looking at the chimney with speculative eyes. "I wonder if we could be searching in the wrong places. Maybe the ring wasn't hidden in the house."

"What do you mean?" Amy asked. "Where else would it be hidden?"

"I was thinking of that hiding place mentioned in the Friends records. You know, where it said that Adam Goodwin's farm had a hiding place for Friends who were being persecuted for being pacifists. I'll bet that's where Adam hid his treasure."

"That's right!" Sara remembered. "When we first read

about that hiding place in the Friends records, I thought so, too."

"Then the hiding place has to be here in the house," Amy spoke up, "because Adam's code message says the ring was hidden in the chimney. And there aren't any other chimneys on the farm that I know of except the ones in this house."

Sam raised his arms and let them flap with resignation against his sides. "Okay, I give up for the time being, but that doesn't mean the case is closed."

Sam never gives up," Sara said, flashing her twin a look of unabashed admiration. "If Adam's treasure is still around here, he'll find it."

With their essays due in a week, no one had to urge them to get busy with their homework after dinner. Sam slipped off by himself, and the girls went to Sara's room to sort through the notes they had collected at the library, from the Goodwin family Bible, and the records of the Friends Meeting.

"I still wish we had Adam's treasure to present with our essay," Amy said wistfully. "Alison will have her ancestor's diary."

"And Doug Cooper his ancestor's handknit sock," Sara giggled. Then she sobered. "But we do have Adam's code message. That should be exciting enough."

She turned her attention to their notes. "When we write our essay, Amy, let's concentrate on the part where Adam discovers the wounded, dying colonel and how, because of his religious convictions, he hides him and cares for his wounds. We could write it in story form, like an exciting adventure, using lots of dialogue and description, like the writers of historical novels."

Amy nodded. "That's a neat idea—sort of dramatize it." She hesitated, her lip curled in a little pout. "I wish it had a happy ending, as most stories have."

"Maybe it'll have a surprise ending," Sara said, smiling mysteriously.

"What do you mean . . ." Amy began.

Sara stared at her with shining eyes. "Like Sam, I'm not giving up on finding Adam's treasure. And if by some chance we do find it, we can write that after all these generations it was Adam's great-great—I don't know how many greats—granddaughter who found the treasure he had hidden. It would sort of be a surprise, happy ending to a sad story."

Amy brightened and her brown eyes looked dreamy. "That would be a terrific ending, Sara."

Encouraged by her friend's enthusiasm, Sara was about to go on with more ideas how to write their essay when there were three short raps on the door. Sam's secret knock.

"Come in," she sang out.

Sam flung open the door and stood there, his face drained of color, his body tensed.

The girls gaped at him.

Sara caught her breath sharply. "What's the matter, Sam?"

Her twin shut the door and took a few steps toward the bed where the girls were sitting, their notes spread out all around them. He swallowed hard, causing his Adam's apple to wobble in his skinny throat. In a tense voice he said, "I just saw the prowlers again!"

11

The Hidden Room

At the word *prowlers* the girls dropped their pencils and shot off the bed in a sudden movement which sent their notes scattering every which way. They grabbed sweaters and followed Sam out of the room.

"Now remember," Sam whispered in guarded tones as they crept down the back stairway, "we don't want to goof off like last time. Let's be sure the kitchen is empty before we make for the side door. And another thing," he warned, "if we want to find out who the prowlers are, we got to sneak up on them. We don't want to scare them off again."

"Scare them off!" breathed Amy in a tense, excited whisper. "They'll more likely scare us."

At the bottom of the stairs they stopped and listened for a

full minute. When they were sure nobody was in the kitchen, Sam gave the all clear sign and they skittered across the room and out the side door.

As they made their way stealthily across the lawn, the night that had closed around them with its protective darkness suddenly brightened as the moon floated from behind a ragged cloud. The yard lighted up as though a spotlight had been turned on them.

Sam flitted like a shadow behind some bushes, and the girls hunkered down behind him, their hearts pounding like hammers in their chests. When, a few minutes later, the moon drifted into another cloud, Sam silently motioned them on.

Keeping well in the shadows of the bushes and trees that lined the driveway, they crept up to the barn. Although darkness covered them again, it seemed to Sara as if the night had invisible, waiting eyes. She felt goose bumps on her arms as she glanced up at the barn which stood before them like a huge black monster, waiting to swallow them up. Trying to curb her racing imagination, she followed Sam and Amy to the door.

As Sam cautiously slid it open, he whispered, "Keep as quiet as you can and follow me."

It was so dark inside the barn that they kept bumping into one another. Sam reached into his jacket for his pocket flash. When he found it, he motioned them on, aiming the small beam of light on the floor and guarding it in the hollow of his hand.

The barn was as quiet as a tomb, Sara thought grimly. There were no footsteps skittering across the stone floor below them, no stealthy movements of prowlers.

"Maybe we scared them off again," she said under her breath, shivering in her light sweater. "Or maybe they're hiding somewhere in a dark corner watching us." The latter thought made her shiver even more.

Sam motioned for his twin to be quiet, and in the frail beam of light they picked their way across the threshing floor.

Suddenly Sam doused his light.

"What . . ." Amy was about to whisper, but Sam put a warning hand on her shoulder.

"Listen!"

The girls tensed, straining their ears. Then they heard what Sam had heard. From somewhere deep in the barn came the sound of muffled voices.

At first they couldn't tell where the voices came from, but by listening closely, Sara thought that the sound came from below them, in the stable.

Sam flicked on the light again, and they moved in a tight knot, step by slow step, to the stairs leading down into the stable. At the top step, they paused again to listen.

Sara stood numb between Sam and Amy, her head cocked to one side, straining to hear what the voices were saying. But all she could make out was a low mumble of sounds.

Sam motioned them on. Warily they made their way down the stairs, the beam from the pocket flash bouncing off each step as they descended. At the bottom they cowered in the darkness as Sam's light bobbed around the stable.

"Nobody's here," breathed Amy. Then the sound of voices came again, stunning them all into silence.

Sam took a step forward, his pocket flash spotlighting the back of the stable from where the sound seemed to come. But there was nobody there, not even in the long shadows that hovered in the corners.

Sam dropped the beam of light to the floor again, and

they moved cautiously across the stable, past the black, grotesque outlines of stanchions that framed the dark stalls, past the mangers and feedboxes. As they approached the back of the barn, the voices seemed to grow louder. And then the talking stopped as abruptly as it had started.

"Where in heaven's name . . ." Sam began.

Sara broke in, "They're on the other side of this wall!"

"How can they be?" Sam's whisper rasped in her ear. "The back of the stable here is built into the hillside."

They turned inquiringly to Amy, whose baffled expression told them that she knew nothing at all about what lay behind the wall.

"Well, let's find out," Sam said in a taut whisper. Boldly he played his light across the gray weathered boards. Sud-

"Maybe they're hiding somewhere in the dark corner watching us," Sara said.

denly a snatch of words made Sara step back in astonishment from the wall right in front of her.

"Those words are coming from behind these boards," she said in a sharp whisper. "I'm sure of it!"

Sam flashed his light on the boards, and at the same moment the voices stopped. The smothered silence that followed made Sara's ears ring.

"How did those voices get behind this solid wall?" Sam questioned in amazement.

"There must be a hidden doorway here somewhere," Amy reasoned.

Sam handed Sara the flashlight, and she focused the beam on his exploring fingers as he ran them over the old boards of the wall.

"There doesn't seem to be anything that faintly resembles a door," Sara breathed.

Sam didn't answer. Now he was pushing his fingers firmly over the boards directly in front of where Sara was standing. His wandering fingers must have accidentally touched a secret spring, for suddenly they heard a click. It sounded so loud in the suspenseful silence that the three of them jumped. A second later a wooden panel swung inward, revealing a small underground room.

Their flashlight raked the darkness of the room, and in one quick glance Sam and the girls noticed that it was lined with gray fieldstone on all sides and had a rough stone floor that gave it the appearance of a small cave. There was just room enough for the frame of a cot, a trestle table with two chairs, and a brick hearth against the back wall. Sara caught her breath as the light focused on the girl and boy who were sitting at the table with a battery lantern and an old book between them. With a little cry of surprise, she took a step forward.

"Alison!"

The girl drew in a quick breath and clapped her hand to her mouth when she saw them staring at her. Her companion scraped his chair back from the table and stood up. He was a stocky boy with broad shoulders and curly brown hair.

When Amy got over her surprise, she exclaimed, "Alison—Pete! What are you two doing here?"

Alison's eyes fairly glistened in the light of Sam's pocket flash, and her mouth made fumbling motions. "I-I'm doing research for my American history essay and—and Pete's helping me."

"In our barn!" cried Sara, unbelievingly.

"Why not?" Alison replied, recovering her composure and tossing back her head. "Didn't Mrs. Bailey tell us to snoop around unlikely places to get original ideas for our essays?"

Amy still looked perplexed. "But what in the world can you find for your essay in this old barn?"

"Plenty," Alison said in a superior voice. She gestured about her. "This hidden room, for instance. It's where Adam Goodwin hid the Quaker pacifists. I'd say it's quite a find and I'm sure the Maplewood Historical Society will agree when they read about it in my essay."

Sam spoke up for the first time. Looking sharply at Alison, he asked, "How did you know about the hidden room?"

Alison pointed to the old book in front of her. "From my ancestor's diary. I'll show you." She snapped on the lantern and thumbed through the pages. She stopped and bent over one of them. "Let's see . . . . Oh, here it is. Major Heston writes: 'I found Adam Goodwin in a hidden room in his stable, where he sheltered Quaker pacifists from being imprisoned. He admitted that he had hidden Colonel Wilkes

105

there, too, so I arrested him in his own barn and took him to the town gaol.' "

She paused and looked up. With a rush of words she explained, "I just had to find this hidden room. I don't think anybody else in Maplewood knows about it, and it would be something original for my essay." She flashed a smile at the boy by her side. "Pete was such a dear to drive me here to hunt for it, and tonight we finally found it. Isn't it exciting?"

Amy gazed wide-eyed around the stone room. "So this is the hiding place that we read about in the Friends' records," she murmured. "And this is where Adam Goodwin had hidden Colonel Wilkes!"

"I hope you don't mind that I found it first," Alison said with a superior smile.

"You may have found this hidden room first," Sara retorted, "but it's still our barn. You could have asked permission to search it, instead of sneaking around like prowlers."

Alison twisted uncomfortably in her chair. "Well," she replied, a slow flush creeping into her face, "since you and Amy are writing about Adam Goodwin, I didn't think you'd want me prowling around on your turf, especially since I am researching how Major Heston caught Adam Goodwin hiding a British colonel."

"You needn't worry about that," Sara said. "We're researching the same thing."

"You are?" Alison asked with surprise.

"Yes, we are," Amy spoke up with a new boldness, "and if you would have asked the Harmons for permission to search their barn, I'm sure they would have given it. Haven't you ever heard of friendly cooperation, Alison? Don't you know that maybe we can help you and you can help us?"

"I don't see how," Alison snapped. "Major Heston and Adam Goodwin had nothing at all in common, and that code I found here wasn't any help. I couldn't break it and neither could Pete."

Sara was taken aback. "Then it was you who stole the secret code from inside my library book!"

Alison's lip curled in an exaggerated pout. "I wouldn't call it stealing. It was more like borrowing. I did return it, you know."

"Don't you ever ask for anything?" Sam said, shaking his head disapprovingly.

"She asks for plenty of rides," Pete groaned. "I don't know how often I've driven her out here. Even had to miss football practice a couple of times."

Sam looked puzzled. "Where did you park the Chevette so that we never saw it?"

"Up the road at the turnout," replied Pete. "Then we hiked through the woods to your driveway."

Alison closed the diary and arose, the chair legs grating harshly on the rough stone floor. She spun around toward the door, but Sam blocked the way.

"Speaking about friendly cooperation," he told her with a crooked grin, "I think Amy has something there."

"What do you mean?" Alison said, her eyes flashing and her voice wearing a harsh edge. "How could we possibly cooperate when I am writing about a war hero and they are writing about a Quaker pacifist?"

"Well, for one thing, I don't think Sara and Amy would mind if you use this hidden room in your essay," Sam said casually, his grin growing wider. "And you sure helped them by finding it."

Sara flashed an inquiring look at her twin. Sam was staring past Alison at the small brick fireplace along the back wall. And then Sara knew what Sam had meant. Another chimney to explore!

"You *have* helped us!" Sara cried. "Oh, Alison, you have!"

The expression on Alison's face was one of blank confusion. "What do you mean?" she demanded.

Sara pointed to the back wall of the little room. "That fireplace," she explained. "By finding this hidden room, you have led us to another chimney."

Alison and Pete looked at Sara as though she had taken leave of her senses. They could only gape with astonishment as the twins and Amy rushed back to the chimney and began what looked like counting the bricks.

"Hey, give a guy a break," Pete said. "Tell us what's going on."

While they searched for loose bricks, they took turns telling Alison and Pete about finding the code message and what it said after they had decoded it. Pete was clearly impressed, and Alison was so excited that a treasure might be hidden in the little room she and Pete had found that they both joined in the search.

"I know we'll find it here," Amy kept saying. "I know this must be the right chimney." Suddenly she gave a little cry and pointed to the two corner bricks at the base of the fireplace. Sara could hear the catch in her voice as she gasped, "There's no mortar between them!"

Sam pulled at the bricks and tried to wiggle them loose, but they wouldn't budge.

"I'll need a hammer and chisel," he grunted.

"I'll run up to Dad's workbench and get them," Sara offered.

With Sam's pocket flash, she was off. When she returned, she handed the tools to the boys.

Pete held the chisel while Sam tapped it gently with the hammer. Finally one brick wriggled loose, then the other

108

one. The girls held their breath as they watched the boys draw the bricks out, leaving a dark opening in the base of the fireplace.

"Is there anything there?" Amy asked in a trembling voice.

Sam peered into the opening. "Hand me the flash, Sara."

Anxiously they gathered around Sam as he beamed the light into the small, dark cavity. Extending his arm into the narrow opening as far as he could reach, he grunted, "I-I think there is something!"

"Well, what is it?" Alison cried, her voice choked with excitement.

Slowly Sam drew out his arm, and they fixed their eyes on the small tin box that he clutched in his hand. He held the box out to Amy. "Here, Amy, you should be the first to open it since it belongs to you and your family."

Amy slowly reached out for the small tin.

"Hurry up," urged Alison. "Open it before I die of suspense!"

With the flush of excitement on her cheeks, Amy tried to open the lid.

"What's the matter?" Sara asked breathlessly.

"I can't open it," answered Amy in a choked voice. "It's stuck."

"Give it to me," Pete said. "I'll force it open with the hammer."

Amy drew back. "No, I don't want the box damaged."

"It's probably rusted shut, being buried in these damp, underground bricks for over two centuries," Sam reasoned. He reached into his jeans pocket, and his fingers closed around his old Boy Scout knife. He drew it out and opening the blades, he said, "Let me have a try at it."

Amy handed Sam the box, and five heads bent intently

over it while Sam expertly scraped the rust away from around the sides with his knife. He wedged the small blade underneath the lid and after wiggling it gently several times, the lid popped open.

They all gasped as they peered into the box. There, nestled in a linen handkerchief, lay a gold signet ring, and the light from the lantern sparkled on the largest diamond any one of them had ever seen.

12

The Winners

For a long moment all five stared at the ring, spellbound. Then Amy's breath caught in a soft gasp and in a stunned voice she murmured, "Oh my...."

The others suddenly found their voices, and Sara heard herself shrilling, "We found it! We found Adam's treasure!"

A low whistle flew from Pete's lips. "Hey, man, you really hit the jackpot! Look at the size of that diamond!"

"Let me hold it," cried Alison, and when Amy put the ring into the palm of her hand, she squealed, "Oh, it's so heavy!"

She passed it on to Sam who proudly displayed it on his middle finger.

After everyone had inspected the ring, Amy wrapped it

carefully in the linen handkerchief and tucked it back into the small tin box. "Let's show it to your mom and dad, Sara," she said.

The five young people trooped up to the house and found Professor and Mrs. Harmon in the kitchen enjoying a cup of tea. They were surprised when the five burst into the house, and they were even more surprised when they saw the diamond ring.

After introducing Alison and Pete to her parents, Sara made some hot chocolate while Sam got some of Mom's homemade sugar cookies from the pantry. Crowding around the kitchen table, munching and drinking, the young people poured out the entire story of their adventures that night. It seemed as though they would never finish, for they kept

Sara heard herself shrilling, "We found it! We found Adam's treasure!"

interrupting one another to add an incident that had been left out.

Professor and Mrs. Harmon listened with rapt attention when they described the hidden room in the stable and told how they had found the diamond ring. Tim, who had come into the kitchen after hearing all the commotion, couldn't help grinning over at Alison and Pete.

"So there really were prowlers in our barn after all!" he said.

Pete grinned back sheepishly. "Sorry we upset you all. I told Alison we should ask permission first."

"I know that now," Alison admitted. She had lost her usual self-confidence and looked a little flustered and anxious in front of Professor and Mrs. Harmon.

Sensing her uncomfortable moment, Sara spoke up, "If it hadn't been for Alison and Pete finding the hidden room in our barn, we may never have found Adam Goodwin's treasure."

"That's right," Amy agreed. "You were a big help, Alison."

A frown puckered the corners of Alison's mouth. After a pause she said thoughtfully, "About that ancestor of Amy's. . . . Why would he help an enemy officer at the risk of being imprisoned?"

"It was because of his love of God and the strong belief in his faith," Mrs. Harmon replied.

Pete snapped his fingers and added, "I get it! Like Jesus preached. Love your enemies."

Mrs. Harmon nodded and smiled. "You summed it up nicely, Pete. Adam Goodwin had to do what he did or he would have been violating that faith."

"But wasn't he . . . afraid of being arrested?" Alison asked.

"Yes, he probably was," Mrs. Harmon said. "But when God is with us and we know we are doing right, we become braver than we thought we ever could be. Our faith sustains us in the end."

Alison was thoughtful as she looked at the diamond ring. With a new tone to her voice, she said, "You really have a family treasure there, Amy."

Amy smiled proudly. "I'm just happy we found the ring after all these years," she murmured.

"And what a perfect place to have hidden it," Sara remarked. "Nobody but Elizabeth knew about the chimney in the hidden room."

"Talking about chimneys," Pete broke in curiously, "you can't see a chimney on the barn from the outside. Where does it come out?"

"Remember, the barn is a bank barn," Professor Harmon explained, "and from what you tell me, the hidden room was built not in the barn itself but into the slope of earth at the back of the stable. So the chimney had to come out on the surface of the ground outside the barn and could have been surrounded by bushes and trees so that it wouldn't be noticed. As the years went by, the top bricks probably crumbled and the chimney itself filled with dirt, disguising it even further."

"What was the fireplace used for anyway?" Alison wanted to know.

"To keep the Quaker fugitives warm whom Adam had hidden in the room," Sam replied.

Sara said dreamily, "I wonder if that old frame cot was the same one Colonel Wilkes slept on while Adam was taking care of him? And was the table the one he ate at and the chairs the same ones he sat on?"

Amy nodded. "They probably were, Sara. They looked

ancient enough." She turned to Alison and there was sudden warmth in her voice. "As Sam said, we won't mind if you and Tracy use the hidden room in your essay. After all, Alison, you were the one who found it."

"Oh, that will be neat!" Alison exclaimed, giving them all a bright smile. "And I promise we won't mention a thing about finding Adam's treasure. That will be your surprise." She paused and let out a wistful sigh. "Just think, a two hundred-year-old treasure to write about!"

The next day, with the tin box safely tucked in Amy's jacket pocket, Professor Harmon drove the girls and Sam to Maplewood. He left Sam off at Kenny Pinto's house, then drove on to the Goodwins. A somewhat sleepy Mr. Goodwin let them in, but when Amy showed her father the diamond ring and told him where it was found, his eyebrows shot up and his eyes opened wide.

"I had given up ever finding Adam Goodwin's treasure," he said with surprise. He took the ring to the window where the light was better and studied it closely. The large diamond glinted in the morning sun.

"Oh my . . ." he exclaimed. "Oh my! I never thought I'd be holding a diamond this size."

He glanced back at them, and Sara saw the haggard look of worry had lifted from his face and he was smiling. "This diamond is worth a small fortune, Amy. We can't keep it here. I'll rent a box at the bank and keep it there until I can get it appraised to sell. With bills piling up, we can sure use the money it will bring."

Amy looked suddenly stricken. "Oh, Daddy, can't we keep it for the American history project?" she begged.

"Sure we can, honey," her father replied, curling an arm around her shoulder. "But even for a short time we should put it in a safe place."

Professor Harmon agreed and offered to drive Mr. Goodwin to the bank on his way to the college. As the girls walked to school, Amy seemed unusually quiet after all the happy excitement. Sara couldn't understand why her friend wasn't bubbling over as she was.

"Why so quiet?" she asked. "We found Adam's long-lost treasure. Aren't you happy it all turned out the way it did?"

Amy agreed with a bob of her head. "Sure I am, Sara. It's just that I wish we could keep Adam's treasure in the family instead of having to sell it." She drew in her breath slowly. "But I know Daddy needs the money real bad."

"Well, that's why Adam hid the treasure in the first place, so that Elizabeth could sell it if she needed money," Sara explained. "I'm sure Adam and Elizabeth would have wanted the diamond ring to be used the same way by a descendant who needed it."

Amy looked thoughtful. "Do you really think so?"

"Of course," Sara said. "Things of value shouldn't be hidden away. They should be used to help others."

"I guess you're right," Amy murmured, her face brightening.

The rest of the week was a busy one for the ninth-graders of Maplewood High. Sara and Amy could think of nothing else but their essay. They soon found out that gathering material about Adam Goodwin, deciphering his secret code, and even searching for the hidden treasure weren't as difficult as the actual writing of the essay.

They spent long hours editing what they had written and then finally transforming their scribbled pages into neat typewritten ones. At last they reached their deadline and handed their essay in. Now came the anxious waiting to find out which essays would win prizes. A committee of three teachers and Miss Finney were to be the judges. They were to read the essays that Mrs. Bailey thought were the best, and then they were to make their decision.

The day before the winners were to be announced, Professor Harmon came home from the college with exciting news. They were sitting around the dinner table when, out of the blue, he told them, "I found a job for John Goodwin."

"Why, that's wonderful," Mom exclaimed. "How did you ever do that?"

Dad leaned back in his chair with a look of satisfaction. "I heard that the college was going to hire a foreman for buildings and grounds; so I went to the business office and talked to them about John Goodwin. They liked the idea that he is a mechanic, and after checking his references, they decided to hire him."

"Wow! That's great!" Sam whooped.

"That's not all," Dad told them, looking mysterious.

"You mean there's more?" Mom said smiling at him.

"The best news of all," Dad replied. "When I stopped by the Goodwins' to tell John about the job at the college, he told me that Amy's mother is coming home from the hospital this week. And when Mrs. Goodwin gets well enough to go out, he is taking his family to church."

Sara stared at her father with surprise. "To our church?"

Professor Harmon shook his head. "No, to the Friends Meeting. He said that after reading the essay you girls wrote, he was so proud of his Quaker ancestor and what Adam Goodwin stood for that he is determined to carry out Adam's faith in this generation."

"Well," Sara said with a happy sigh, "if our essay doesn't go any further than that, it has accomplished a wonderful thing."

"It surely has," her mother agreed.

The next day a special assembly was called to announce the winners of the American history project. Sara and Amy marched into the auditorium with the other anxious ninth-graders. On her way to her seat, Sara glimpsed Alison and Tracy sitting together, their eyes glued to the stage. Sara noticed that Alison didn't look quite so sure of herself as she had the day she announced to the class that she and Tracy would be writing about her famous ancestor, Major Heston.

A hush settled over the assembly as Mr. Epily, the principal of Maplewood High, arose to speak. Sitting next to him on the stage were Mrs. Bailey and Pastor Reese. Mr. Epily adjusted the microphone on the podium then cleared his throat several times before he began to speak.

Sara fidgeted while the principal explained at length how the Maplewood Historical Society wished to keep alive the history of Maplewood by sponsoring the American history project. He praised the efforts of the students in Mrs. Bailey's social studies classes and said that the essays were so good that the judges had a difficult time selecting the best ones and regretted that not everybody could win a prize.

Sara held her breath as he introduced Pastor Reese, president of Maplewood Historical Society. She was sure now that the winners of the American history project would be announced. But no. The high school band struck up a patriotic tune, and the anxious ninth-graders had to sit through two more selections before Pastor Reese finally arose and walked to the podium.

With a great deal of care he adjusted the microphone to his own level, put on a pair of horn-rimmed glasses, and placed a sheaf of papers on the podium. To the anxious Sara, his actions seemed to be made in slow motion. At last he spoke, greeting Mr. Epily, the faculty, and the students of Maplewood High.

Amy reached for Sara's hand and held it tightly while Pastor Reese looked at his papers for the names of the winners of the best essays.

Her hand in Amy's, Sara squeezed her eyes tightly shut. Her head was spinning. It was as if she were miles away from this auditorium and that she was hearing a blurred voice from a long way off calling her and Amy's names.

At first she thought she was imagining it. Mom always said she had the most vivid imagination in the family. But when she opened her eyes and saw everyone turning in their seats and smiling at her and Amy, she knew she had not imagined it at all. She had actually heard Pastor Reese call out their names.

The next moment Mrs. Bailey was motioning them to the stage to receive first prize for the winning essay. Sara could feel her cheeks burn as she arose from her seat, but Amy didn't seem at all ruffled. She was absolutely radiant as they stepped up on the stage together.

Pastor Reese shook their hands and smiled at the two girls. "The reason the judges give for choosing your essay is that you have unearthed another kind of hero in Maplewood," Pastor Reese explained as he handed them both the check for $50. "Very few people now living in Maplewood know who Adam Goodwin was and that he sacrificed his life for his religious beliefs and for his compassion for an enemy soldier. We are grateful to you for letting us know about him, and we are proud to have him listed as one of Maplewood's heroes."

A thunderous applause filled the auditorium. But Sara only half heard it as she stepped down from the stage. It was Sam's proud smile in the front row that caught her attention and made her feel warm inside.

When the applause subsided, Pastor Reese read the

names of the winners of the second prize, and Sara was happy to see Alison and Tracy walk up to the stage. The third prize winners were two boys from Sam's homeroom.

On the way out of the assembly, Doug Cooper pushed through the crowd and caught Sara by the arm. He was all smiles as he congratulated her and Amy.

"Meet me by your locker after school, Sara," he said hastily before leaving them. "I want to ask you something." And without saying another word, he disappeared down the crowded hall.

Amy rolled her eyes at Sara and smiled. Sara blushed deeply and wondered what in the world Doug wanted to ask her that had to be asked in private. He certainly was acting mysterious.

It seemed that the last class would never end. When the buzzer finally sounded for dismissal, Sara hurried down the hall to her locker. She was surprised to find Doug already there, leaning against the locker door, waiting for her. It wasn't until he was walking her to the school bus that he asked, "How about going to the get-acquainted party with me Saturday night, Sara?"

Sara looked up at him with surprise. "The get-acquainted party?"

"Sure, Maplewood High has one every fall in the gym," Doug told her. "Wow, Sara, where have you been? Everyone's been talking about it."

Sara gave a little apologetic laugh. "I guess I've been so busy living in Adam Goodwin's world that I didn't hear about it. I'll ask Mom and Dad, but I'm sure it'll be okay. I'll let you know tomorrow, and thanks for asking me."

The school bus was about ready to pull out when Sara breathlessly boarded it.

At dinner that night, Sam told about the assembly and

how proud he was that Sara and Amy had won first prize for the best essay in the American history project.

"Amy did most of the writing," Sara said modestly. "She's a much better writer than I."

"Yeah, but it was your idea to write about Adam Goodwin," Sam reminded her. With his crooked grin he added, "You know, Twinny, this is the first time you got a better grade than I. Things are looking up for you."

Mom and Dad smiled proudly at Sara, and Tim gave her one of his special winks. Sara thought this would be a good time to approach the subject of the get-acquainted party.

"Um—this boy in my homeroom—Doug Cooper—asked me to go to the get-acquainted party at school on Saturday night," she put in quickly.

They all stared at her as if she had never gone to a school affair with a boy before.

Tim came to her rescue. "That's swell, Sara. Vickie and I will be there." Turning to his parents and assuming the role of older brother, he added, "We'll drive her to the gym and keep an eye on her."

Sara fumed inwardly. She was grateful to Tim for assuring Mom and Dad that everything would be all right. But he didn't have to keep an eye on her. It wasn't her first date and he knew it!

Sam spoke up just then. "Do you have room for two more in that jalopy of yours, Tim?"

Immediately her family forget about Sara and turned to Sam with surprise.

Sam blushed and grinned. "Hey, what's the big deal? Can't a guy ask a girl for a date?"

"Who did you ask?" Sara wanted to know.

Sam looked away quickly. "I haven't gotten around to it yet," he admitted.

"Well, who are you thinking of asking?" Tim probed.

Sam colored deeply. "Amy Goodwin."

"Amy?" shrilled Sara. "Oh, Sam, that's super!"

"Un huh," Tim wagged his head at his brother and smiled knowingly. "I saw how you looked at Amy the first night she came here for dinner. I said to myself, 'Old Sam is really falling for a girl at last.' "

"Do you think she'll go with me?" Sam looked desperate.

"Of course she will," Sara assured him, her eyes dancing. "All you have to do is ask her."

"Maybe I'll call her tonight," Sam pondered. "I believe I'll do a better job asking her over the phone than at school in person."

They all laughed, then Dad reached over to put his hand over Mom's. "Honey, our children are growing up."

Mom smiled wistfully. "Yes, dear, I know."

Tim drove them all to the get-acquainted party on Saturday night. It was a close fit in his VW, but they didn't mind. Sara thought it was more fun to arrive at the school gym in her brother's old jalopy than to have her father drive her.

During the last couple of days she and Amy had planned carefully what they would wear to the party. Amy's father, who had started working at the college, gave Amy money to buy a new outfit, and Sara helped her shop for it.

Vickie had offered to give Amy a home perm, and the sandy wisps of hair became soft curls that gave Amy's sharp-chinned face a cute, pixy look. Sam's eyes fairly popped when he met her at her door the night of the party. Then, composing himself, he proudly escorted her to the VW.

Doug was already at the gym when they arrived. After Sara introduced him to Vickie and her brothers, they mingled with a group of kids from their grade.

Doug was as easy to talk with tonight as he had been between classes at school. He introduced her to all his friends, and Sara no longer felt like the new girl at Maplewood High.

When they all got together again at the punch stand, Alison sauntered up with Pete and invited them to her house for something to eat afterward.

"Hey, you're in!" Doug teased when the others wandered off.

Sara smiled as she looked in the direction of Amy and Sam. "I don't particularly want to be 'in,' " she answered happily. "I just want to be friends with everybody."

"That's what I liked about you from the beginning," Doug whispered in her ear. "It's sure great to know that there are girls like you around."

Hand in hand they walked around the gym, and Sara never felt happier.

Ruth Nulton Moore lives in Bethlehem, Pennsylvania, with her husband who is a professor of accounting at Lehigh University. They have two grown sons and a granddaughter.

Specializing in English literature, she received a BA from Bucknell University and an MA from Columbia University. She did postgraduate work in education at the University of Pittsburgh.

A former schoolteacher, Mrs. Moore has written for *Children's Activities* and *Jack and Jill*. She is author of twelve published novels for children, among them, *Danger in the Pines*, which won the *Christian Schools* magazine's C. S. Lewis Silver Medallion, and *In Search of Liberty*, which received the Silver Angel Award from Religion in Media. Her books have been translated into Swedish, Finnish, German, and Spanish and sell in England,

Puerto Rico, and Canada as well as in the United States.

Mrs. Moore is a member of Children's Authors and Illustrators of Philadelphia, and her biography appears in *Contemporary Authors*, *The International Authors and Writers Who's Who*, and *Pennsylvania Women in History*. When she is not at her typewriter, she is busy lecturing about her art of writing to students in the public schools and colleges in her area. She also does volunteer work for her church.